The Bootlegger's Wife

Denise Devine

USA Today Bestselling Author

A Sweet Historical Roaring Twenties Novel

Moonshine Madness Series – Book 1

Wild Prairie Rose Books

The Bootlegger's Wife

(Moonshine Madness Series - Book 1)

Print Edition

No ghostwriters were used in the creation of this book. This story is the original work of Denise Devine.

ISBN: 978-1-943124-13-8

Published in the United States of America

Wild Prairie Rose Books

Edited by L. F. Nies and J. A. Dalton

Cover Design by Raine English

Also available as an audiobook

Want to stay in touch with me? Visit my website at https://www.deniseannettedevine .com or sign up for my newsletter at https://eepurl.com/csOJZL and receive a ***free novella***. You'll be the first to know about my new releases, sales, and special events.

To my maternal grandparents,

Charlotte Esther Smith and William Charles Van Elsberg,

and to

my brother, Ken, my biggest fan,

who called me nearly every day, waiting for me to finish this book so he could read it.

~

5-stars – 2019 Readers' Favorite International Book Awards

(The Bootleggers Wife)

Denise Devine has written this book with a really good plot and characters that become real. The conclusion is too good to share but it is a must-read to find out the twists and turns that occur. I highly recommend The Bootlegger's Wife be added immediately to your reading list. You won't be disappointed.

-Trudi LoPreto for Readers' Favorite

Chapter One

May 15, 1925

It was a typical Saturday night of drinking, dancing, and defying the law at La Coquette, the newest and most luxurious venue in St. Paul, Minnesota. Tuxedos, silk gowns, and diamonds described the dress code of our clientele; "anything goes" was the name of the game. From sparkling chandeliers and oriental carpets to white linen tablecloths and fine china, the enormous success of our ritzy nightclub exemplified a dream come true for Gus and me.

Gus handled the business end of La Coquette. My job was to welcome special guests and impress them with our hospitality. Some of our guests came from North Dakota or Chicago, clients who purchased liquor through our bootlegging operation. Others were corrupt city officials who accepted bribes to look the other way.

Patrons had their choice of a casino in the basement, a supper club on the main floor, or private rooms on the upper level for business meetings and invitation-only card games. Except for invited guests, everyone paid at the door for a ticket to eat, drink, and be as merry as their hearts desired. As far as the drinking part went, we served the setups—a glass with ice and ginger ale—and our customers spiked the drinks with their own supplies of bootlegged liquor. The club employed several off-duty policemen to watch over the crowd, but as long as customers were discreet about their liquor consumption, the police left them alone.

The guests at my private table made up an impressive list of St. Paul's finest public servants, all on my husband's payroll. Tonight, Gus and I had invited four couples to meet us for cocktails and dinner. To my dismay, Gus had stayed for one cocktail then excused himself for an appointment and never returned. It was unlike him to be so rude and it irritated me. If his meeting had detained him indefinitely, he could have at least dispatched Albert, his right-hand man to let me know so I could make his apologies to the group. I didn't feel well and hoped to take my leave early, but Gus' disappearance put me behind the eight ball. Unfortunately, I didn't have the strength or the energy to search for him and talk him into coming back to the party.

On my right, the wife of a police sergeant stood and raised her glass for a toast. A buxom redhead with a quick smile and a hearty laugh, Sally Wentworth looked like the cat's meow in her aqua silk and cashmere dress with a gold skirt sash wrapped around her hips. A hairclip stuffed with peacock feathers clung to the thick finger waves above one ear. "Come on everybody. Here's to a generous hostess and a great gal to boot." She turned to me and smiled. "You're the bee's knees, Charlotte LeDoux. You know how to put on one heck of a party."

As everyone agreed and touched the rims of their glasses together, she bent low and whispered, "And if my instincts are correct, you're expecting, too. Congratulations! I won't say anything until you announce it yourself. Does Gus know? He hasn't mentioned it."

Shocked by her statement, I stared at her and shook my head. I hadn't told a soul yet, not even my husband. I'd had so many miscarriages in the past, I didn't want to get Gus' hopes up until I knew for sure I wouldn't lose this one, too. "How did you know?"

Sally sat down and placed her hand over mine. "I've been in your place a few times." She patted my hand. "Honey, you're whiter than those beautiful gloves you're wearing and you look so exhausted I'm worried you might collapse and fall off your chair. The first few months are always rough, but it'll get better. You just make sure you get enough rest."

"As a matter of fact, I—"

A waiter appeared at my side and before I could wave him away, he placed a glass in front of me filled with ice, ginger ale, and a shot of whiskey from Gus' private reserve. "Mrs. LeDoux, you need a refreshment. Shall I bring one for Mr. LeDoux as well?"

My stomach roiled as I looked down at the glass. The sharp aroma of "Minnesota 13," reputedly the best corn whiskey in the country, wafted into my face. At this point, I didn't care if it was the best whiskey in the universe, I couldn't stand to look at it without fighting off a wave of queasiness. I closed my eyes and pushed it forward. "Please, Gordon, take it away. I don't care for anything tonight."

Or ever again if it continues to bother me this much...

Sally snatched the glass and held it to her lips. "I'll take it. No sense wasting good hooch." She tossed it back and handed the waiter the empty container. "Thank you, Gordon."

Then she turned back to me. "Keep a bowl of soda crackers next to your bed. It helps with morning sickness. A glass of lemon-lime soda occasionally might settle your stomach, too."

I thanked her and groped for my silvery-blue shawl and matching mesh purse. The fringed bag, designed by Coco Chanel, contained a hundred dollars in small bills, a tube of red lipstick, my powder compact, and a small, pearl-handled revolver. Gus insisted I carry the revolver with me always, even though I detested guns. I would have traded it right now for a handful of crackers...

"I need to find Gus," I said weakly and pushed back my chair. I needed to escape before I embarrassed myself by fainting or vomiting all over my beautiful, silvery blue gown. What little I managed to eat at dinner threatened to come back up.

"You look awfully pale," Sally said, frowning with concern. "Perhaps I should come with you."

Though I understood her concern, I didn't want company. I just wanted to find my husband and go home. Clutching the rope of pearls around my neck, I placed my other hand on the table for support and shakily rose to my feet. "Thank you for asking, Sally, but I'll be fine."

"All right, but you go straight home now and take care of yourself."

I promised her I would as she straightened my shawl and sent me off with a hug. Waving goodbye to my guests, I headed across the smoky room in search of Gus. As I made my way through the crowd, the room began to spin and I immediately regretted not accepting Sally's aid. Though in my third month, my pregnancy had plagued me all along with bouts of fatigue, nausea, and dizziness. Afraid of falling, I quickly clutched the back of the nearest chair to keep my knees from buckling.

An older gentleman with thinning hair and a bushy mustache turned toward me, surprised by my intrusion. My face must have shown my distress for he frowned and placed his hand on my elbow. "Miss, are you all right?"

I wanted to collapse on the floor and bawl my eyes out, but instead, I mustered a faint smile. "It's so warm in here...I just need to get some fresh air."

I concentrated on staying upright as I slowly walked away, determined to find Gus and make him take me home. At the next table, I stopped one of our cigarette girls, a slim blonde with a chin-length bob wearing a short red dress and matching pillbox hat. She roamed from table to table, carrying a tray of cigars, cigarettes, and novelties for sale. "Irene," I said evenly, attempting to mask my desperation by sounding merely curious, "have you seen Gus?"

"No, Mrs. LeDoux." Irene shrugged. "I haven't seen him since Madame Deveraux arrived."

Adrienne Deveraux—our newest singer and the most evocative performer I'd ever witnessed. A raven-haired beauty, her smoky voice, hourglass curves, and poisonously scarlet lips oozed with sensuality. From the moment she'd cast her dark, sultry eyes on Gus, I knew she'd set her sights on him. I had a sinking feeling she had her red-lacquered claws into him at this very moment.

Scanning the cavernous room, I searched for Gus, but I had difficulty focusing on the person next to me, much less the sea of people hopping like chickens on the dance floor. Every night, the revelers would dance the Charleston in front of our twelve-piece orchestra until the early hours of the morning. On the weekends, we entertained them with popular musicians and a twenty-five-member dance team that performed a new show every Friday. Tonight, the raucous, drunken crowd caroused as though they hadn't a care in the world as they waited for the show to begin.

Frustrated, I turned my back on the reverie and slowly made my way toward the stairway that led to Gus' office on the upper level. I clung to the railing and pulled myself up the stairs, my head pounding in sync with every step I took.

At the top of the stairs, I paused to get my breath. After a few moments, I made my way down the hallway, leaning against the wall for support. At the end of the corridor, I turned the corner and encountered Albert Schmidt, Gus' personal bodyguard. The short, dark-haired man looked formidable with thick arms, a stocky build, and the strength of an ox. He stood guarding the door to Gus' private office, a Colt 1911 automatic pistol gripped in his right hand. My greatest fear turned out to be true. Gus had stationed his paid watchdog at the door so no one would interrupt him. Even an idiot could guess why.

By now, nausea and dizziness plagued me so heavily I could hardly stand, but I mustered all the energy I had to look the big German square in the eye. "I need to talk to Gus. *Now*."

Albert pushed back his black Fedora with the tip of his gun. His deep voice held a trace of his native accent. "I got strict orders from da boss. No one is to disturb him. *No one*."

A low, passionate moan seeped under the door of Gus' office.

Under normal circumstances, I liked Albert, but I didn't care for him very much right now. Mustering up the strength to stand up straight, I poked him square in the center of his starched white shirt. "Listen, you big goon—I mean what I say." Placing both hands on his chest, I tried to push him away. "Move away from the door, mister, and that's an order."

His face blanched, but I knew it had more to do with his embarrassment of my hearing Gus' lover in the throes of passion than the threat of my knee in his groin. He didn't budge. "I cannot do that, Frau LeDoux."

The guttural sounds coming from under the door angered me so much I temporarily ignored my condition. I had worse things to deal with now. I started to pull the revolver from my handbag, hoping the sight of it in my palm would show this hired thug I meant business. "Step aside, Albert. This is between Gus and me!"

I probably looked as ridiculous as I sounded, but Albert didn't laugh. With a stoic face, he calmly but firmly pulled the revolver from my hand and proceeded to empty the bullets from the gun's chamber. "I mean no disrespect, but I'll keep these."

Citizens of the underworld were fearful of my husband and called him "boss" or "sir." When I seethed with anger, as I did now, I called him every swear word I knew. And after nine years of marriage to Gus, I knew them *all* in his native language of French as well as in English.

"I know you're in there!" I screamed in frustration as I ripped off my gloves and threw them at the door. "You and your French whore!" Since I couldn't get past Albert, I resorted to the only thing a girl could do to disarm a man. I began to sob. Given my condition, the emotional outburst came easily. "Come out, you coward—right now—and face me! How dare you treat me like this!"

I figured the tears and calling my husband a coward in public would be enough to get his attention, but the door stayed shut. Holding my stomach, I glared at Albert and said in a shaking voice, "I want my bullets back."

He slipped the bullets into the pocket of his navy suit coat and handed me the empty revolver. "Calm down, Frau LeDoux. Be a good wife and go back to your guests." He put his hand on my shoulder and gave me a sympathetic look. "There's nothing you can do about it."

Angry at Albert's ridiculous and insulting suggestion, I pushed his hand away. "If Gus thinks I'll simply go away and keep my mouth shut, he's crazy. I will never accept this—"

Suddenly a door at the far end of the hallway slammed open and one of the machine gun-toting sentinels from the catwalk on the roof burst into the hallway. "It's a raid!" he hollered as he tore past us to warn the people downstairs. "Get out fast! The Feds are coming!"

My hair stood on the back of my neck. My arms filled with goosebumps. The one thing every bootlegger feared had come upon us…

The door to Gus' office flew open and my husband stood in the doorway holding his machine gun, his sandy hair as disheveled as his wrinkled white shirt. His suspenders hung loosely at his sides. He showed no inkling of remorse at being caught literally with his pants down.

Behind him, Madame Deveraux eyed me with a sly, triumphant smirk as she pulled up the straps of her ruby silk gown.

My emotions flared red-hot at her brazen gesture. I was tempted to

11

scream insults at her, but when I looked into Gus' cold, sage eyes, I realized she was a byproduct of our failing marriage rather than the cause. For months, the demands of managing La Coquette had left precious little time for Gus and me to share the intimacy we'd once had, and I'd hoped the news of my long-awaited pregnancy would begin to draw us closer again. Obviously, it was too late. Gus had become infatuated with Adrienne Devereaux.

I took in the scene before me and deep in my soul, something irrevocably changed. My belief in true love and "happily ever after" with this man had shattered. I knew I'd never trust him, or any man, with my heart ever again.

"Get her out of here!" Gus glared at me but spoke to Albert. I knew Gus was deadly serious when he offered his new "Tommy Gun" to his bodyguard. "You know what to do."

Albert slipped his handgun into his shoulder holster and took possession of the machine gun. "Yes, boss." Jumping into action, he pulled me down the hallway. His vise-like fingers locked on my arm, the other hand gripped his ten-pound Tommy Gun. "Come with me, Frau LeDoux."

"No!" I fought with all my might as Albert dragged me away. "Let go of me!"

"Take her down to the hollow, Al." Gus glanced over his shoulder at Adrienne then back at me. "I'll get there as soon as I can—"

The piercing of sirens arriving at the building cut him off. Everyone froze at the cracking of gunfire.

Gus' eyes blazed. "I said *GO!*"

At the top of the stairs, Albert slipped his free arm protectively around my waist and hauled me down to the main floor, shielding me with his rock-hard body as he muscled his way to the coatroom through the screaming, thundering mob. Behind a movable rack of fur wraps, a small group of employees was filing into a tunnel through a secret door in the paneling. "Coming through. Step aside!" Albert pulled me to the head of the line and pressed his broad palm against my shoulders as he guided me through the door. In the tunnel, the men who'd gone ahead of us carried flashlights to show us the way.

The musty, dank passageway, filled with cobwebs and centipedes gave me chills, but after what I'd just witnessed, I knew I fared much better than the people in the club. Gripping the edges of my fringed shawl, I marched along the downward slope, keeping up with the others. I had to escape for the sake of my baby. The thought of being arrested and taken to jail frightened me to the core, but it also strengthened my resolve to keep going, no matter how badly I wanted to stop and catch my breath.

As we approached the end of the tunnel, I recognized the Katzenbaum brothers just ahead of me. Marv, stiff from arthritis, hobbled along with a large ledger tucked under each arm. He'd served as the chief bean counter for Gus' father back when the family brewery was in operation, but now he worked for us. Harv, Gus's attorney and also a long-time employee of the LeDoux family, carried a sack of money in each hand.

The tunnel ended at the bottom of a hill, surrounded by a thick stand of oak trees and shrubbery. Once we reached the exit, we passed through an open door into the twilight. Relieved to have fresh air, I stopped and inhaled deeply, but the frightened screams of a panicked mob and roaring sirens back at the club spurred me on. Albert and I picked up the pace again.

"Where are we going?" I hollered as we emerged from the trees to a city street. I saw the auto dealership directly across from us and knew we were headed there. Gus and I owned it.

Albert grabbed my hand, pulling me along as we ran across the street to the car lot. We passed between used Chryslers, Chevrolets, and

Packards until we came to a new Nash Touring Car. Its black exterior would make it harder for the Feds to see us, and if Albert chose it as his getaway car, it had speed, too.

Suddenly, a man in a dark suit sprung from behind one of the cars holding a gun. "Stop! You're under arrest—"

Before the agent finished shouting, Albert shoved me away, raised his gun with both hands, and shot the man multiple times.

I couldn't believe what was happening. My head swam with terror. I bent at the waist and covered my ears to keep my head from ringing, but it didn't help. Bullets discharging from Albert's weapon created a blast so loud the force literally shook my body. When the bullets finally stopped, my legs buckled and I slowly collapsed to the ground. As I lay on my side, I saw the agent lying prone a few feet from me. I smelled the sickening, coppery odor of blood. My mouth began to fill with saliva…

Albert ripped open the car door and wrapped his arm around my waist, lifting me off the pavement. "No!" I struggled to get away as fear and revulsion overtook me. Seeing what he was capable of, I couldn't stand the thought of his hands touching me now. "No! Get away from me!" I didn't have anywhere near the strength I needed to match his. As a last resort, I began to cry. "Please, Albert, let me go!"

"Get moving!" He forced me into the front seat, slammed the door, and cranked the car to start it. We were leaving by the back entrance of the lot as a torrent of bullets whizzed past us.

Bracing my shaking hands against the dash, the stench of burnt gunpowder constricted my throat and made my eyes water. I hung my head, coughing. The scene back in the parking lot flashed through my mind again like a bad dream.

Oh, my God… I-I've just witnessed a murder…

Albert's large, rough hand pressed on my shoulder. "Get down!"

Numbed by my thoughts, I slumped to the floorboard as Albert gunned the gas pedal and drove like a maniac, dodging parked cars and speeding through intersections. Without warning, he made a quick turn and the car nearly slid out of control. I hung on for dear life. My tummy problems didn't seem important anymore.

Dear God, please get me out of this alive! I beg of you, spare my baby!

Still concentrating on the road, Albert flattened his palm on the empty seat. "Take these! Put them back in your gun." On the seat lay the bullets he'd removed from my revolver. I really didn't want them back, but the ugly growl of his voice frightened me into action. I obediently scooped them up and stuffed them into my handbag. After the horror I'd just witnessed, I could *never* shoot anyone.

A short time later, I poked my head above the dashboard, thinking I would be safe now that darkness had descended. "How much longer until we reach the hollow?"

"Never mind. Stay down!"

Albert drove through a dark tunnel at breakneck speed into the deep ravine called Swede Hollow, a little hamlet of shanties without electricity or running water. I'd grown up in the hollow and even though my family had long ago moved to a better neighborhood, I still knew some of the families living there. Before Prohibition had shuttered its doors, my father had worked at the LeDoux Brewery, situated on the edge of the ravine; the same place where I'd met my husband, Rene Gustav LeDoux, the eldest son of the owner.

Just when I thought we'd escaped the Feds a torrent of bullets showered the car. The back window shattered and Albert slumped over the wheel.

"Albert!"

The car careened out of control. Still on the floor, I slammed my head against the seat as the car bounced over rocks along the marshy bank of Phalen creek and came to an abrupt stop. For a moment I sat hunched over, gasping for breath, aching badly. Slowly, I raised myself above the dashboard and realized my thigh hurt fiercely in one spot— where I'd been sitting on my purse with my gun still in it. I pulled my silvery beaded hat and dropped it on the seat. My necklace caught on the shift stick. Dozens of Japanese pearls scattered across the floorboard.

"Albert? Albert, what's wrong?" I reached over and cautiously touched his arm.

His lifeless form suddenly slumped against the door. Gasping in horror, I scooted away.

A flash of headlights cut through the dark, moonless night as several cars sped out of the tunnel. I grabbed my handbag with one hand, clutched my shawl with the other, and scrambled out of the car, dropping my feet into the cold stream.

Unnhhh...

Shivering uncontrollably, I waded through the ankle-deep water, slipping on rocks until I reached dry land and hurried toward a narrow footbridge that led past a row of outhouses built on stilts over the creek. Shielded from the oncoming headlights by the line of buildings, I stumbled across the bridge, desperate to get away before the men on my trail caught up to me. Once I'd made it safely across the creek, I hobbled into the brush and made my way behind a small, darkened house. My mind couldn't think straight, but gut instinct warned me to keep putting one foot in front of the other.

The screech of brakes cut through the air, indicating cars had come to a stop somewhere along the creek. Several doors banged successively as the agents jumped out to investigate the scene.

"Don't look back," I whispered to myself and forced my feet to move faster, knowing the Feds would apprehend me unless I found a good place to hide—or slipped away into the night. Using the back of my hand, I brushed my hair from my face, leaving something sticky on my cheek. My fingers had suffered a long, horizontal cut, most likely from a piece of flying glass. Oddly enough, it didn't hurt.

I quickly approached my former childhood home, a tiny, weathered shack, wishing I could stop there and rest awhile. My right hip ached like crazy, but I knew I couldn't stop until I'd reached the western slope and the tall wooden stairway that led to the sandy road above the railroad terraces.

A chorus of shouts indicated people were already coming out of their houses to see what all the ruckus was about. Though Gus was counting on it, I had decided not to ask anyone for shelter. Within minutes, the Feds would be all over this place, searching for me and I didn't want to risk getting any of these good people in trouble for harboring a fugitive. Besides, with the Feds so close on my heels, I didn't have time to find out if anyone *would* help me.

As I hurried through the inky darkness in sloshy T-strap shoes and a wet dress, I gradually felt no discomfort, only a strange sense of calm. Pulling my shawl tighter around my shoulders, I thought about what I'd do next. I had no idea where my husband was—in jail perhaps or...dead. Knowing Gus, he was still alive. He hadn't earned the nickname "Lucky LeDoux" for nothing. To my astonishment, however, I didn't care one way or the other. I only knew that I couldn't live this life anymore—as a bootlegger's wife.

The thought of leaving Gus terrified me, but at the same time, it gave me a sense of hope for my baby's future. Sadly, I knew better than to believe things could go back to the way they were before Prohibition when Gus worked in his father's brewery. Once the Volstead Act passed—the eighteenth amendment—the LeDoux Brewery had been forced to shutter its doors, destroying the family income and causing his father, Rene Sr. to suffer a fatal heart attack. Gus' deep-seated anger at the government for devastating his family and the folks who'd depended upon the brewery for their livelihood had fueled his decision to forge ahead despite the risks. Enlisting many of his former employees, he'd formed a new operation bootlegging Minnesota whiskey and operating La Coquette.

Now, he was a criminal, wanted by the Feds…

Before Prohibition, Gus and I had lived a simple life as an ordinary couple and we were happy together. Nowadays he preferred collecting barrels of money and spending it on women and other sinful pleasures more than he loved me. Even so, he'd never let me go if he discovered I planned to leave him—especially in my present condition. This I knew without a doubt.

Albert's lifeless form flashed through my mind and I shuddered, wondering if I would ever feel safe again. My eyes smarted with tears. I couldn't bear the thought of subjecting my child to the perilous life my husband had chosen.

I had two choices—locate Gus and live in constant danger or start a new life for myself and my unborn child. Casting apprehension and excuses aside, I told myself I needed to follow my instincts and do what would be best for my baby. It didn't take long to choose my path.

Charlotte LeDoux had ceased to exist.

Chapter Two

June 19, 1925

At ten o'clock in the morning, I stood on the sidewalk in front of a huge, colonial revival house on Laurel Avenue, contemplating my future. It had been over a month since I'd escaped the raid on La Coquette. Since then, I'd been living in a cheap rooming house in quarters no larger than a postage stamp, but in much better health now due to a lot of rest. Unfortunately, I'd nearly run out of money and needed to find employment. I'd used most of my remaining cash to have my dark brown hair trimmed and dyed red with henna. My pearl earrings and evening ensemble had been sold to purchase a plain navy shift, matching cloche hat, and flat Mary Jane shoes. Wire-rimmed glasses and a freshly washed face without makeup completed my new disguise.

The advertisement in the *St. Paul Pioneer Press* for a "live-in" housekeeper/cook listed this address and instructed candidates to apply between 10 am and 4 pm. As I studied the gray, three-story mansion with white trim, I wondered who lived there. Situated in a quiet neighborhood in St. Paul, the house stood like a fortress, shrouded by tall, majestic trees and flanked by houses of equal stature on both sides. Now that my sickness had passed and I could work, I needed a place such as this to spend my days tucked away, safely hidden from society. For now, anyway.

Clutching the small satchel that held my few belongings, I walked toward the house. A ruby-throated hummingbird buzzed my head as I passed between twin cement urns filled with scarlet geraniums in full bloom. At the top of the steps, I opened a wooden gate and walked across the wide, wraparound porch to a screen door. Behind that was an inner door with a long, oval glass window. With nervous anticipation, I placed my satchel at my feet and twisted the doorbell. It made a loud *br-r-r-ing*. I waited, but no one answered. My apprehension mounting, I tried the doorbell again.

Perhaps they've already filled the position and the occupants are simply ignoring me...

Surely, my logical mind reasoned, if they'd already hired someone, they would have posted a sign on the door to discourage anyone else from bothering them.

I wanted this job. No, I *needed* this job, desperately, so I had no choice but to persist until someone opened the door and spoke to me.

Glancing through the small oriel window on my left, I caught a glimpse of an ornate wooden staircase leading up to the second floor. Along the wall hung a large portrait of a regal woman and farther up, the morning light brightened a stained-glass window. At the top of the staircase, the steps curved to the right. I squinted to see if I could spot anyone coming down to answer my ring, but it appeared as though everyone was either occupied or out of the house at the moment.

Stubbornly, I twisted the doorbell one last time.

The rapid tapping of footsteps on a wooden floor approached the inner door. When it opened, I found myself staring through the screen door at the face of a tall, slender woman. The smoothness of her taut skin indicated she might be in her middle twenties—the same as me—but her pale coloring and mousy hair bound into a tight chignon at the nape of her neck made her look older. Her brown, floor-length skirt and high-necked, cream blouse with long sleeves were of good quality, but woefully behind the times.

Narrowed green eyes peered at me as she stood in the small corridor between the inner and outer doors. "No soliciting!" She pushed open the screen door a couple of inches and shoved her hand out, pointing to the metal plate below the doorbell. "Can't you read the sign?"

I straightened and drew in a deep breath. "I'm applying for the housekeeper position."

She shook her head with annoyance, as though one glance at me told her all she needed to know. "I need someone with *experience*."

I stared back at her. "I have experience."

Our gazes locked for a tense moment then she looked me over in one fell swoop, appraising me with disdain. "You're wasting my time. I don't employ *flappers*."

Given the woman's outdated mode of dress, her attitude didn't surprise me in the least.

She didn't like flappers, I surmised because they were independent and free-spirited women. Traditionalists—like her—considered the flapper lifestyle outrageous and immoral. Flappers were known to drink, smoke, voice their opinions, and wear their skirts short to show off their legs when they danced. Due to my condition, I couldn't stomach smoking, dancing, or drinking anymore, but being in the family way didn't have any effect on my tongue. Desperate or not, I had a mind to tell her what I thought *of her* when she suddenly turned and walked away.

"Louisa?" Inside the house, heavy footsteps accompanied a man's voice as he approached the door. "Is someone here about the job?"

She walked back into the foyer. "Yes," she answered him in a voice much sweeter than she'd used on me, "but she didn't meet the qualifications. I've sent her away." She shut the door.

Exhaling a disappointed sigh, I picked up my satchel and walked across the porch. There was a corner soda shop a couple of blocks away on Selby Avenue. Squandering my last ten cents on a strawberry ice cream soda would soothe my disappointment while I sat in the booth and scoured the "Help Wanted" section of the newspaper for another job opening.

The front door suddenly creaked open. "Miss?" The deep, masculine voice projected a friendly, but curious tone.

Halting at the top of the steps, I slowly turned around. A tall, broad-shouldered man with black hair, possibly mid-thirties stood in the doorway wearing black pinstripe trousers and a matching vest. His starched white shirt, open at the neck and rolled up at the sleeves, gave me the impression he'd been busy working on something before the doorbell interrupted him. A leather holster strapped to his left shoulder held a pistol just below his armpit.

"Yes?" I waited, equally curious. He must have gazed through the large bay window in the front parlor and observed me standing at the door.

"Good morning," he said amiably, but with an air of authority. "I'm Will Van Elsberg."

"I'm Esther Smith," I replied, using my middle name and my mother's maiden name.

The crown of my head was level with his shoulder. He gazed down at me, his intense blue eyes studying mine. "Are you here about the housekeeper position?"

"Yes, I am…I mean, I was, but…"

"Excellent. What prior experience do you have?"

More than you can imagine. I operated a successful nightclub for a year…

The woman suddenly appeared behind him. "Will, I've already spoken with her and she's not suitable—"

"Thank you, Louisa, but I'll handle this," he remarked smoothly and stepped onto the porch.

Excited at getting a chance to be considered for the job, I stood ramrod straight and clutched my satchel with both hands. "I worked at Finnegan's Hotel for two years while I was in school. It's near the cathedral."

The breeze blew a lock of his thick, wavy hair across his forehead. He ignored it and nodded, indicating he knew of the place. "What were your duties?"

"It's a small, family-operated business so I learned several jobs," I replied. "I started as a cook's helper in the kitchen then I learned to operate the front desk and after that, I got promoted to housekeeping."

"How experienced are you at preparing meals?"

"I'm an excellent cook." That was true, but other than supervising the chefs at La Coquette, I hadn't spent much time in my own kitchen in the last several years. Once the builders finished constructing our new home, Gus and I had employed people to handle the domestic duties for us.

"And you have references?"

My head bobbed with enthusiasm. "I can obtain a written reference from Finnegan's today."

"Where have you worked since then?"

My mind whirled, searching for a plausible answer to his question. A place where I wouldn't be able to produce a reference…

"I haven't worked anywhere," I suddenly blurted. "I've been home, taking care of my ill mother. She has a heart ailment." That was true about my mother, but I hadn't needed to give her care for several years. Once Gus and I could afford it, we'd hired a nurse to check on her several times a week.

Seemingly satisfied by my answer, he stood to one side and opened the door, ushering me inside with a sweep of his hand. "Come in. I'll show you around the kitchen."

I walked into a long foyer with a high ceiling, dark woodwork, a wood floor, and a long parlor table against the wall along the stairway. The cut flowers in the vase on the table were brown and crispy—they'd been there so long; the table and green art deco lamp were coated with a layer of dust, giving me cause to wonder how long the household had gone without domestic help.

To my left, the grand staircase ascended to the second floor. To my right, I observed the front parlor with dark red drapes and a matching room-sized rug, but instead of the usual furniture, the room held two large wooden desks. One had a telephone sitting on it and the other held a shiny black Underwood typewriter. There were also several side chairs, wooden file cabinets, and a marble-topped parlor table. I wondered what type of business took place in that room, but didn't ask.

We passed through the dining room, though I failed to notice much about it. A putrid odor coming from the kitchen assaulted my nostrils long before we walked into the room. Someone had set a fan by the back door to draw the offensive fumes through the screen, but it did little, if any, to relieve the problem.

Slipping my satchel on my arm, I covered my nose and mouth with my hands. "Oh, my goodness, what is causing that smell?"

He spun around, placing his hands on his hips. "I have no idea, but it's driving me crazy. I was hoping you could locate the problem and take care of it."

"Yes, sir." I pulled off my hat, dropped my satchel, and brushed past him, heading for the Frigidaire. It had to be coming from there. However, when I opened the main door, I found a sealed bottle of milk, a container of fresh eggs, several wrapped packages of cheese, butter, and bacon, but no spoiled food. Scratching my head, I looked around. It smelled like something was dead…

"I'll leave you to it," Mr. Van Elsberg said and walked out of the kitchen.

"Why didn't *she* take care of this?" I murmured to myself, hard-pressed to understand why his wife would simply put a fan at the back door instead of trying to get at the root of the problem.

After a few minutes of unsuccessfully poking around in the drawers and cabinets, I stood with my arms folded, racking my brain over what to do next. I couldn't stand much more of that disgusting odor. Nausea was beginning to slowly creep up the back of my throat.

Follow your nose…

The scent seemed to be stronger near the floor. I got down on my hands and knees and crawled around, finding it the strongest by the Frigidaire. Bracing my hip against the huge wood-paneled box, I pushed as hard as I could, but it only moved a couple of inches. That was enough. Peering between the appliance and the wall, I spied a dead, rotting mouse.

Ugh. Now I truly wanted to vomit.

Snatching the newspaper from my satchel, I ripped off a large piece and slipped my hand behind the Frigidaire, scooping up the slimy little critter. Outside I went, holding my breath and making a beeline for the waste container.

Back in the kitchen, I rummaged around in the cabinets until I found a box of baking soda and a drawer with scrub rags and kitchen towels. In less than ten minutes, I had the smelly area wiped down and odor-free. Then I began filling the dishpan with fresh hot water and Lux soap flakes to tackle the rest of the mess.

The kitchen had the shiny new look of a recent modernization with a brown and white tile floor, an electric stove, a new sink, and the newest model of Frigidaire. The sink, however, overflowed with dirty dishes. A couple of pans with burned or scorched food were piled up on the stove. Judging by the stream of ants marching across the counter, they had been there a while. What a shame. Again, I wondered, how could anyone allow this mess to accumulate in such a wonderful room?

"Ah, the air is much better in here now," Mr. Van Elsberg said, walking through the doorway with an empty coffee mug as I stood at the sink scrubbing crusted food off a plate.

"It was a decomposing mouse." I pointed to the area where I'd located it. "And your dishes are covered with ants."

He glanced at the china draining in the metal rack. "You do good, fast work. I'm impressed by the way you took charge of the situation and went above and beyond the task I gave you. The job is yours if you want it. The salary is twelve dollars a week and you'll get paid every Friday."

Relieved, I stopped and wiped my hands on a towel. I didn't have enough money for a hotel room or even a hot meal. Hopefully, I'd be occupying a bed in the servant's quarters tonight. "When do I start?"

He flashed a disarming smile. "You already have."

The rapid tap-tap-tap of footsteps into the kitchen interrupted the moment. "Will, I've just interviewed a woman who has the qualifications we're looking for," the person he'd called Louisa said in that sickly-sweet tone she'd used once before. "An older lady with years of cleaning and cooking experience. She's waiting in the parlor for you to speak with her."

"Give her my apologies." He walked over to the stove and grabbed the coffee pot. "I've already hired Esther."

She blinked. "You...hired *her*?" She glared at me with disapproval, as though the blame for his decision to retain such an upstart like me was somehow mine. "But, Will, we need someone *proper—*"

"Louisa," he said gently, but firmly as he poured himself a cup of coffee. "I've made my decision."

Pursing her lips into a pout, she crossed her arms and stomped out of the room.

The disagreement between them made me uncomfortable. I placed my towel on the counter. "I apologize, Mr. Van Elsberg, for upsetting your wife. Perhaps I should leave. I don't want my employment to cause division between the two of you."

"Don't worry about that, you're not," he replied with a frown. "Louisa Amundsen is my secretary, *not* my wife." He lifted one brow. "And I thank God every day I *don't* have one."

Well, that answered one question that had been lurking in the back of my mind since he'd stepped out to meet me on the front porch. No wonder they were like night and day. Her stiffness and old-fashioned ways didn't strike me as the type of woman he would even want to associate with socially much less marry.

His dry wit made me smile. I liked this man immensely, but I understood his secretary's concern over the inappropriateness of having a young female employee living in his house. Propriety, however, was the least of my worries. Staying safely out of the crosshairs of my husband and the Feds mattered a lot more.

Mr. Van Elsberg walked over to the Frigidaire and opened the main door. "There isn't much in here, but can you make me something to eat? I'm starving. I've been living on sandwiches for days."

So, he was responsible for the burned pans…

"If you don't mind eating breakfast for lunch, I could fry some bacon and eggs and whip up a batch of pancakes."

He nodded and handed me the stoneware mug. "Make some fresh coffee, too."

*   *   *

The sharp, staccato notes of the keys on Miss Amundsen's typewriter echoed throughout the house as I made lunch for her and Mr. Van Elsberg. They sat down together in the dining room, nibbling on crisp bacon as they discussed the morning's work. I thought it odd that he would eat a meal with an employee, but I kept my opinions to myself and went silently about my duties, serving the food and eventually removing plates and refilling coffee mugs and water glasses. That was my present goal; to go about my job as quietly and unobtrusively as possible. Living in this house would give me the anonymity and the money I needed until I could figure out where to go from here.

After lunch, Mr. Van Elsberg donned his suit coat and hat and left the house.

Miss Amundsen walked into the kitchen carrying a bundle of clothing. "These are your uniforms," she said and walked past me. "Make sure they're clean and ironed before you wear them, starting tomorrow." She heaped the ball of wrinkled garments on the counter and pulled a handwritten piece of paper from her pocket. "Here are the menus for the week. Breakfast is at seven, lunch is at noon. Mr. Van Elsberg usually goes out after lunch to work on his cases and often has dinner with clients so he will be gone until late. There is a market a couple of blocks from here on Selby Avenue where you'll get food supplies every Monday. Mr. Van Elsberg has an account there. They'll deliver the goods sometime that afternoon. You also need to drop off his shirts at the laundry next door and retrieve the laundered ones. You'd better make a trip this afternoon." She raised a critical brow. "He deserves a better lunch than eggs and bacon."

I started to ask her a question, but she turned and walked away. As my words trailed off mid-sentence, she suddenly stopped at the doorway. "Your room is on the third floor." She gestured toward the narrow stairway in the rear of the kitchen leading to the upper floors. "*Always* use the back staircase. But then, since you're *experienced* you should know that along with what your duties are. You get Wednesday and Sunday afternoons off."

I nodded obediently. "Yes, Miss Amundsen."

Then she was gone.

My arms were wrapped around the heap of uniforms, aprons, and headbands when the basement door behind the servants' stairway opened up and a strange man in denim overalls walked into the pantry, startling me.

"Hello, are you the new housekeeper? I'm Daniel Blythe," the husky, red-haired man said. His thick mustache stretched into a wiry fringe across his face when he smiled. He held out his hand to shake. "I keep the place in good working order."

I set the ball of clothing back on the counter and shook hands with him. "I'm pleased to meet you, Daniel. I'm Esther Smith and yes, I'm the new housekeeper."

"Welcome! I'm happy to hear that. It's been a while since we lost the last one." He gestured toward the coffee pot on the stove. "Can you spare a fella a cup of joe?"

"Yes, sir," I said jovially and pulled a white stoneware mug from the cabinet. "It's still fresh from lunch. How long has it been since the last housekeeper left?"

"At least a week." He accepted the steaming cup. "An older gal. She didn't see eye to eye with Miss Amundsen. Said she would only take orders from the man of the house, so Miss Amundsen fired her." He sighed. "Most don't last long around here. Did she explain my arrangement with Mr. Van Elsberg?"

"No." I leaned against the counter to stay upright as fatigue began to slowly seep through my limbs. "She never mentioned you at all."

He took a loud sip of hot coffee. "I handle all of the property maintenance, including gardening. I also keep an eye on the place whenever Mr. Van Elsberg is out. Besides my salary, I live rent-free in the rooms downstairs and get two meals a day."

No wonder he's happy to see me. He's probably starving...

I laughed. "Then why didn't *you* dispose of the dead mouse before the smell got so bad?"

"Been gone for a couple of days visiting family. Just got back."

"So, tell me," I whispered, changing the subject as I glanced toward the kitchen door to make sure no one else overheard me, "what is Mr. Van Elsberg's profession?"

"He didn't tell you?"

"No, he didn't get a chance. Miss Amundsen interrupted our conversation."

Daniel took another slurp of his coffee. "He's a private investigator."

"You don't say. That must be an interesting business."

"Oh, yes." Daniel's green eyes twinkled with a knowing look. "There's never a dull moment around here."

That sparked my curiosity and I wondered how he knew so much about our employer's clients if he spent most of his time working. "What kinds of situations does he investigate?"

"Insurance fraud, cheating spouses or business partners, runaways, missing persons—"

A chill went down my spine. My head began to swim. I gripped the counter for support.

"Easy there." Daniel set down his cup and gently grasped my upper arms to hold me upright. "What's wrong? Aren't you feeling well?"

I took a deep breath, hoping he hadn't realized just how much his words had affected me. "Just tired, that's all."

His worried expression softened. "Rough first day, huh?"

I nodded. "I haven't worked in a housekeeping position for a few years. It's going to take me a while to get used to it again."

My shoulders sagged with fatigue and for a moment, I worried this job would prove to be too strenuous for me. I planned to turn in as early tonight as possible to get a good night's rest. In the meantime, I still had errands to run and a uniform to launder and press. Hopefully, taking in the fresh air on the way to the market would clear my head.

Miss Amundsen said Mr. Van Elsberg ate dinner out most nights. I desperately hoped he had plans to stay out tonight. I doubted I'd have any strength left to cook him dinner if he decided to spend the evening at home.

Daniel let go of me and grabbed his mug off the counter. "Well, I'd best be on my way and let you get to it." He held up his mug. "You make good coffee."

"Thank you," I said as I picked up the pot and gave him a refill. "I'll have breakfast ready for you at seven."

"Seven it is." He headed for the back door. "Don't hesitate to ask if you need anything. All right? I'm here to help."

"I'll keep that in mind."

It lifted my spirits to know I had an ally in Daniel Blythe and I had a feeling I'd be asking him for more help than he'd bargained for.

Chapter Three

Miss Amundsen left for the day at five o'clock. I assumed she must live close by as I watched her leave the house by the front door and travel on foot. She approached "Holcombe Circle" at the end of the block, a small roundabout filled with greenery and a wooden park bench, turning the opposite way she would have gone if she had intended to catch the streetcar.

Mr. Van Elsberg returned late in the afternoon to make a few phone calls then went upstairs to change for the evening. He came back downstairs wearing a tuxedo and informed me that he wouldn't be home until late. As soon as his blue Chrysler backed out of the small driveway behind the house, I finished putting away the grocery order then headed for the servant's stairway. I wanted to see the bedrooms before I went to the top floor to find my own sleeping arrangements. With my satchel in hand, I climbed the stairs to the second floor to view the layout and see what cleaning needed to be done.

There were four bedchambers with transom windows above the doorways and a large lavatory on this level. I wondered if the rear room had been the master bedroom in the past for it had a smaller chamber attached to it. The extra room could have served as a nursery at one time because it contained a window and a separate entrance, but now sat empty. I peered inside the little room, hoping I had a special place like this for my baby after it was born.

Farther down the hallway, I found a large bedroom on my left, a smaller bedroom on my right, and an airy, sunny room with a bay window facing the street. All of the quarters were unoccupied except for one; a large bedroom that obviously belonged to Mr. Van Elsberg. Situated on the east side of the house, it was the shadiest of all the rooms. The breeze coming through an open window felt comfortable, despite the heat of the day.

His room looked neglected with dirty shirts draped over a chair and the bedclothes piled in a heap on the large, four-poster bed. For the most part, however, my employer was a tidy man—starkly different than my husband who simply pulled off his clothes at night and dropped them to the floor, leaving them for me or the maid to pick up the next day. I glanced around the room, expecting to find a lost earring, perhaps, or a cigarette butt tinted with lipstick, but no such clues were evident. Either he didn't have a current girlfriend or he spent his romantic evenings elsewhere.

As tired as I was, I dropped my satchel and went about straightening the mess. Tomorrow, I told myself, I'd do a thorough cleaning of the entire floor, but for tonight, at least it was presentable.

After that I wearily trudged back to the stairway and climbed to the third floor, panting for breath as I reached the top. The sweltering air on this level shrouded me like a damp cloak, thick with dust and a strong musty odor. The main hallway, like the floor below, stretched from end to end, but this floor had slanted ceilings, much smaller bedrooms, and more storage rooms. To my surprise, I found the perfect place to settle. The cozy little room was sparsely furnished with a small dresser and an urn-shaped lamp with a parchment shade. A narrow bed was nestled between twin dormers with rounded arch windows that looked down upon the street. I promptly pulled back the curtains and opened both windows to let in some fresh air.

The bare, faded mattress sagged from wear, but that didn't deter me. I was grateful simply to have something to rest my weary body upon. After slipping off my flat, Mary Jane shoes, and my glasses, I lay down with a grateful sigh. My body relaxed at once, my eyelids fluttering as my cheek sunk into the soft folds of a worn and yellowed feather pillow. The faded blue curtains billowed in the light, summer breeze; the rustling of leaves in the trees and the warble of a songbird formed a natural lullaby that beckoned me to drift into a much-needed sleep…

* * *

The slamming of car doors and peals of shrill, youthful laughter pulled me out of my dream-filled state. I awoke with both a terrible thirst and the need to use the lavatory, two things that had plagued me constantly since I'd become pregnant. I had no idea what time it was, or whether the gray shadows in the room were the product of twilight or the dawning of a new day. Slowly, I rose to a sitting position and sat quietly with my eyes closed until my grogginess gave way to clearer thinking. The call of nature became more urgent as the minutes passed, forcing me to stand and slowly stagger out of the room. Eventually, I made my way to the lavatory on my floor—the only one I was allowed to use. Through a small window, the last pinkish rays of the evening sun were nearly gone, giving way to the starry expanse of an indigo sky.

The clock chimed nine times as I descended the staircase in the kitchen to help myself to some ice water from the Frigidaire. I turned on the light and selected a drinking glass from the cabinet.

Feeling refreshed, I walked into the foyer and turned on the lamp, curiously observing the simplicity of my surroundings while I sipped my chilled water. The atmosphere in the house took on an entirely different tone at night. Without Miss Amundsen's palpable tension, the telephone ringing, and Mr. Van Elsberg's booming voice, the rooms generated a peaceful serenity I found most enjoyable.

Not ready to go back upstairs yet, I wandered into the living room and turned on a floor lamp. High walls painted a soft green were paired with a cream ceiling. A darker green, high-pile rug covered the floor. A davenport and matching wing chairs upholstered in green were positioned to face each other in front of the fireplace.

I picked up a green and rose striped accent pillow and thought about my own home—the luxurious palace-like mansion on Summit Avenue with oak archways, a wall-length fireplace, and a sunroom I would never step foot into again. Did I miss my old life? The house Gus had built for me was grander in size and more fashionable than this one in every way, but I had never experienced the peace in my own home that I felt here. In this house, I could fall asleep without fear of waking up to gunfire and Federal agents breaking down the doors. I didn't have armed bodyguards trailing me everywhere I went or patrolling the property around the clock, making me feel like a prisoner in my own home. I expelled a sigh of relief. I had no second thoughts about leaving my wealthy—but dangerous—life behind and returning to the simple, pragmatic existence I had before Prohibition began—

The front door suddenly swung open and slammed against the woodwork. "Hello?" The female voice sounded a bit perky and too loud, as though she'd been imbibing more than her share of bootlegged whiskey. "Is anybody home?"

My heart jumped to my throat. Who would be dropping in to see my employer at this time of night? A girlfriend, perhaps?

Hiding my empty glass behind an easel-style picture frame, I spun around and stepped into the softly lit foyer. A tall, slender woman of about my age, maybe a little older, with short black hair stood in the doorway wearing an orange silk dress. The knee-length garment was sleeveless with silver and gold beaded embroidery. A silver shawl draped crookedly across her shoulders.

"Mr. Van Elsberg is out for the evening and I'm afraid he didn't say what time he'd be back," I said politely. "Would you like to leave a message for him?"

Leaving the door open, the woman walked into the foyer and made a dismissing wave with her hand. "Not necessary. I'll talk to him later." She pulled off her orange cloche hat and shook her head, fluffing her chin-length curls. "Who are you?"

"I'm his housekeeper," I replied, confused. Why would she ask that? Then I remembered I wasn't wearing a uniform.

Her kohl-lined eyes gave me an appraising once-over. "You must be new."

"Yes, ma'am. I started today." I clutched my skirt. "Please excuse the way I—"

"I'll bet the bluenose didn't hire you, did she?" Her generous orange-red lips formed a wry smile. "She only hires *old* women. They're no competition for Will's attention."

The…who? I blinked, stunned by her frankness.

"She's in love with him, you know. He barely notices her." The woman arched a finely-penciled brow. "The only reason he hired Louisa was because our dearly-departed mother asked him to help out the daughter of an old, family friend. The job was supposed to be temporary to give her some experience and a reference while she looked for permanent employment, but then Mother passed away and Louisa took it upon herself to slip into the role of managing the household. That's when I moved out."

The woman opened her crocodile handbag and pulled out a cigarette. "This subject is depressing. I need a drink." She expelled a tense sigh as she smacked her handbag on the parlor table and lit the cigarette. "Do you know where Will keeps his hooch stashed nowadays?" Without waiting for an answer, she pulled up her skirt and drew a small flask from her garter. "Ah, never mind. This'll do."

"Yes, he did hire me," I said, warming up to her. "He's a very nice man."

"That he is, but I'm probably biased because he's my brother." She took another drag off her cigarette and tipped her head back, blowing the smoke toward the ceiling. "I'm Madeline, by the way."

I smiled. "I'm Esther."

Madeline frowned. "You sound familiar. I feel like I know you from somewhere. Did you ever work for the Carlson family?"

My heart began to pound frantically. She had probably seen me walking through the main area at La Coquette, randomly stopping at tables to visit with customers. "No." I shook my head with too much vigor, at the same time, realizing I'd forgotten to put my glasses back on. "No, this is my first job in domestic work in a long time."

Someone in a car parked in front of the house leaned on the horn.

Madeline shrugged and glanced toward the doorway. "Sounds like my friends want to get back to the club." She capped her flask and slipped it back into the garter hidden under her dress. Then she grabbed her handbag and started for the door. "No need to tell Will I stopped by. I don't want any lectures on the company I keep. I'll give him a call tomorrow—after five o'clock." Resting her hand on the doorframe for support, she stopped and looked back. "Goodbye, Esther, and good luck with the bluenose. A girl as pretty as you will need it in *this* house."

* * *

The next morning, I dressed in my uniform consisting of a black gown hanging nearly to my shoe tops, and a white apron with scalloped edging that formed a "V" across the front and tied at the waist. A black ribbon headband trimmed with white ruffles held my chin-length hair back. The dress hung like a sack on me, but I didn't mind. The baggy garment would be useful in hiding my tummy once it started to swell. For now, my pregnancy didn't show, but my waistline had increased. My mother always said, "Boys were carried toward the back; girls were all out front." If her predictions were correct, my child was a boy. However, I didn't have time to ponder that now. I had a huge house to clean and meals to prepare.

While making breakfast, I came upon an old cookbook in a drawer. Curious, I flipped it open and the volume parted to a well-worn page, dog-eared from much use and dusty with flour; a recipe for a cinnamon coffee cake. My mouth watered at the thought of warm, sweet cake, and coffee for breakfast. Someone had made this particular recipe many times, so I surmised it must be good. I thought it would make a nice addition to breakfast for everyone.

When Daniel, our resident handyman, arrived for his oatmeal and coffee, I presented him with a slice, still warm. His eyes grew wide with surprise. "Well, thank you." He grasped a small pitcher, drenching the cake with fresh cream. "Hmmm…." he said as he picked up his fork and speared a moist chunk. After a moment he smiled. "I haven't had cake this good in a long time. You're the bee's knees, Esther."

His compliment reminded me of my friend, Sally, whom I'd frequently had dinner with at La Coquette. I swallowed hard, trying not to let the traumatic ending of our last evening together spoil my mood. I wondered what had happened to her during the raid and it made me a little sad to know I'd probably never find out.

Mr. Van Elsberg poked his head into the kitchen. "Is that coffee cake I smell?" At my nod, he rubbed his palms together and said, "Good. I'm looking forward to it."

I set his place at the head of the dining room table. Miss Amundsen took the place to his right, a deep frown etching lines in her forehead as he pushed in her chair. She wore another drab outfit today, a brown dress with puffy sleeves.

I poured the coffee then returned from the kitchen with a plate containing several warm pieces of cake.

She stared unhappily at me. "Where's our breakfast?"

"It's ready, Miss Amundsen."

She pointed to the plate in the center of the table. "What's this?"

"Cinnamon coffee cake."

"Was it on the menu I gave you for today?"

I hesitated. "No, ma'am."

She glared at me. "Then take it away."

Embarrassed at having displeased her, I reached over to retrieve the plate, but Mr. Van Elsberg placed his fingers lightly on my wrist, stopping me. "Leave it here." His blue eyes held mine but conveyed no emotion. "That will be all, Esther."

"Yes, sir."

I scuttled back into the kitchen. Daniel had heard the exchange and met me with a sympathetic look. "She's in a foul mood today," he murmured. "I'd better leave before she comes into the kitchen and catches me eating a piece." At my urging, he helped himself to another piece before he picked up his dishes and headed outdoors to eat on the back step.

I finished dishing up the entrees then hurried to serve the meal. Mr. Van Elsberg dug into his food immediately, but Miss Amundsen sat ramrod straight, staring at the coffee cake to let me know that my enthusiastic burst of creativity—without prior permission—had stepped over the line and touted her authority.

No one spoke to me through the meal, even though I bustled around the table, removing plates and refilling coffee. Mr. Van Elsberg consumed his food with remarkable speed and stood up to leave the dining room, taking his full mug with him. "When you're finished, Louisa, I have a few items I'd like to go over with you."

"Certainly," she replied softly as she stood. "I'll be right there."

I removed their plates and escaped to the kitchen. To my dismay, Miss Amundsen followed right on my heels…

She charged into the room with the serving plate in her hand and dumped the leftover cake into the waste bin. "From now on, you will make what is on the menus I provide and *nothing else.*"

"But I thought—"

"You're not being paid to *think,* Esther. You're being paid to work. You'll do as you're told or the next time, you'll find yourself out on your ear. Do I make myself clear?"

"Yes, ma'am," I said obediently, though inside my temper simmered at the pettiness of it all. For the last three years I had run a household and eventually managed a huge nightclub, handling problems left and right, and through all that time I had *never* treated anyone in the cruel, derisive manner she treated me. Mr. Van Elsberg had wounded her pride by hiring me against her objections. Since then she'd made it her mission to belittle and humiliate me until either she found cause to fire me or I simply gave up and left on my own accord. I vowed to avoid her as much as possible until I decided it was time to leave on my *own* terms.

She slammed the plate on the counter. "Now get back to work. I want every inch of this house cleaned *today.*"

In stony silence, I turned away and began washing dishes.

At ten o'clock, Mr. Van Elsberg wandered into the kitchen and found me thumbing through the old cookbook, looking for a recipe to make the dish Miss Amundsen had listed on the day's lunch menu. He strolled over to the coffee pot on the stove and helped himself to a refill. I'd just made a full pot and the strong, fresh-brewed aroma must have enticed him. "Say, is there any of that cake left?"

The loud tapping of Miss Amundsen's typewriter echoed through the house. I breathed a sigh of relief, happy she couldn't hear our conversation. "You're in luck." I opened an upper cabinet door. "I have two pieces." In truth, I'd deliberately set them in a saucer and hidden them away for Daniel's mid-morning coffee, but if Mr. Van Elsberg wanted them, I'd find something else for Daniel to eat.

He helped himself to a piece and contentedly devoured it, giving the impression he wasn't in any hurry to get back to work. "So, you found Minnie's cookbook," he said pleasantly after he'd swallowed the last bite of cake and drank half of his coffee. "She'd been the family cook since I was a kid. Unfortunately, she passed away last year, a few weeks before my mother did."

"I'm sorry to hear that." I set the saucer on the counter, wondering if that had anything to do with why he ate out every night. "My condolences on the loss of people close to you."

"Thank you. I miss them both, including Minnie's cooking."

"Judging by the wear on the pages, she must have used it every day. Perhaps this belongs with you." I carefully closed the book. "If it's a family keepsake—"

"Not at all." He gave me a generous smile. My stomach fluttered but it wasn't because of the baby. "I *insist* you keep it here and put it to good use."

"Do you have any favorite dishes you'd like me to make?"

He shook his head. "Surprise me."

I suddenly realized my error. "I'll do my best within the bounds of the menus I've been provided. As you know, Miss Amundsen requires me to strictly adhere to them."

"Don't worry about that," he said with a wink. "I'll take care of it."

"Will, there is a phone call for you." Miss Amundsen stood in the doorway. Her tone of voice held that sugary lilt she manufactured whenever she spoke to him. It irritated me. "*In the parlor.*"

He turned his back to her as he refilled his cup. "We'll talk again later," he said casually to me and set the pot back on the stove. Without a word to Miss Amundsen, he brushed past her and went back to the parlor to speak to his caller.

She stood frozen, her hands clenched at her sides as she glared at me through narrowed eyes, livid because I had the nerve to bypass her and discuss my issue with Mr. Van Elsberg directly. "Overstep my authority again and you and *I* will talk, as well."

What a drab, insecure woman, I thought, watching her turn around and storm away. She reminded me of a mean hen in her brown outfit and hair twisted into a tight knot behind her head. I didn't like her, nor did I fear her, either. Even so, I knew she was waiting for the first opportunity available to get rid of me. Mr. Van Elsberg had intervened this time, but I needed to watch my step and avoid her as much as possible.

Later that afternoon, he returned after being out for several hours. I assumed he'd be gone for the rest of the day, but I was upstairs dust mopping the hallway when I heard raised voices coming from the parlor. Though I couldn't make out the words, the shrill tone of Miss Amundsen's replies caught my attention and as I leaned against the mop, I wondered if my day of reckoning had already come…

Chapter Four

My suspicions were correct. The conversation between Mr. Van Elsberg and Miss Amundsen centered on me, though the outcome surprised me.

Not only did he refuse to allow my dismissal for disobeying her rules, but he also informed her that, starting immediately, he expected me to follow Minnie's tradition and plan the meal menus myself. A small victory; nevertheless, Miss Amundsen retaliated by refusing to talk to me for the rest of the day. I didn't understand why until Mr. Van Elsberg told me of the change in my duties that evening, just before he went out.

"You have full run of the kitchen," he said to me in a serious tone. "As long as the food is good and on the table on time, I don't care what you make. Once in a while, I'll have a few friends over in the evening and I'll ask you to make something special, but I'll let you know in advance. If you run into any problems in the course of doing your job, you come to me, understand?"

"Yes, sir," I replied in amazement, realizing he'd just informed me that I answered to him from now on and if his secretary interfered, to let him know. I sensed there was more to it, but didn't ask.

I spent my first afternoon off resting in my room. I was too tired to go out anyway, even for a walk. I didn't have any money, so I decided to lay on my bed and page through the cookbook. In between naps, I composed my grocery list. I liked my cozy little room with double windows. It gave me a wide view of the street. Though the summer heat often made the room very warm, I loved the peaceful, quiet atmosphere up there and I got a bird's eye view of everything going on in our little stretch of neighborhood. Best of all, I was hidden away here. And for the first time in years, I felt safe.

On Sunday afternoon, I finalized the menus for the week and constructed a grocery list.

On Monday morning, Miss Amundsen was absent at breakfast. When I casually inquired about it, Mr. Van Elsberg told me—without looking up from his morning paper—that she would be starting her workday at eight o'clock from now on and therefore wouldn't be joining him for breakfast. By keeping his nose buried in the paper, he missed the brief smile on my face as utter surprise swept through me. Then relief. I'd never witnessed him reading the paper at the table before and formed the opinion he'd tired of such formal rules, including the woman who enforced them.

Later that day, I made my weekly trip to the market and the laundry but on my way back home I stopped for an ice cream sundae at Big Louie's, the neighborhood soda shop. Lately, as the weather had turned hotter, I'd begun to crave all things cold. If they were sweet, so much the better. Miss Amundsen would be watching the clock closely, so I had to eat fast, but once I tasted the frozen concoction, it didn't take long to devour it.

I scraped the bottom of the sundae glass with my spoon, wishing the treat hadn't disappeared so fast when a movement in the front window caught my eye. I looked up and saw Daniel peering in. Embarrassment and guilt burned my cheeks at being caught indulging myself when I should be working. He waved and quickly headed for the entrance. Once inside, he removed his hat and walked toward my booth.

"Fancy meeting you here. Mind if I sit down?"

I stood. "I can't stay. I've taken too long already. Miss Amundsen is probably waiting for me to return."

He slid into the booth, laid his flat cap on the seat, and gestured for me to take my seat again. "Tell her the market was busy today and it took longer than you anticipated. I'm supposed to be at the hardware store, picking up plumbing supplies." He grinned and pointed toward my empty sundae glass. "What did you order?"

Hearing he had no intention of reporting me to my employer, I smiled and sat down again. "Moonbeams—the special of the week. It was made with everything I love, vanilla ice cream, marshmallow crème, shredded coconut, and chopped walnuts." He grimaced at the mention of coconut, so I added, "Next time I might try the Cherry Royal. Do you come here often?"

He nodded and pulled the menu from behind the sugar dispenser. "A couple of times a week I stop by for an early dinner. They make good ice cream here, but they also have other excellent food, like sandwiches and soup. The other day I had spiced rhubarb. Almost as good as my Ma used to make."

"I'll have to try it sometime." I slid out of the booth and grabbed the package with Mr. Van Elsberg's laundered dress shirts. "I'd love to stay here with you, but I'd better get going or Miss Amundsen will reprimand me."

He looked up. "Have a good day. I'll see you later."

"Okay!" I waved goodbye and hurried out of the soda shop. I walked briskly all the way home, thinking about all the chores waiting for me...

*   *   *

There were only two people who knew I was still alive—my mother and my sister. They were the only individuals I could trust with

45

my secret. I didn't get the chance to check in with them until the following Wednesday. I had my first week's wages in my handbag, minus the ten cents I'd spent treating myself to ice cream at Big Louie's. I wore the navy dress, but it was beginning to feel tight all over and I knew I would have to get another one very soon. My hat fit snuggly on my head and I pulled it down to the rim of my glasses, hoping my head covering helped mask my true identity.

When the streetcar arrived at my stop on Selby Avenue, I dropped six cents into the farebox, asked for a transfer, and took a seat. With my head down and my eyes closed, I sat resting until the conductor announced the Seventh Street line. At the corner, I exited and ran to catch my connection on the opposite side of the street. The car was full, forcing me to stand until I disembarked at Maria Avenue on St. Paul's east side. From there, I walked several blocks to my mother's home on Fifth Street.

When I first left Gus and was staying at the rooming house, before I found my housekeeping job, I used to come at night to visit my family. Now that I had to work every day, I had no choice but to come during my afternoons off. I was taking an awful risk going to Mamma's house in broad daylight, but there was *no way* I was going to stop seeing them.

Fearing Gus might have someone watching the house, I cut through neighboring backyards, nervously looking over my shoulder. I darted from one outbuilding to the next, scanning the area for cars parked in the alley, especially expensive ones—the kind Gus liked to drive. As a wanted man, he'd be taking a serious risk watching this neighborhood on a regular basis, but I knew him; he'd find some way to take that chance if he thought it would lead him to me.

Once I reached Mamma's house, I took one last look around then went in through the back door.

Gus and I had always provided for Mamma and my sister. Papa had contributed nothing for years. He was an alcoholic who often disappeared for months at a time. When he did show up, he'd help himself to food and confiscate whatever money Mamma had before leaving again. Gus and I wanted to move her and my sister into our home and take care of them, but Mamma begged us to let her stay in her own place.

Mamma had been ill for as long as I could remember. Sadly, her heart had grown weaker with each passing year and even though she was now bedridden, she desperately wanted to keep what little independence she had. I understood what a terrible strain it would be on her to change her accommodations against her will, so Gus and I respected her decision and let her remain in her home. I'd visited Mamma several times since I left Gus, but due to a lack of funds, I hadn't been able to come home for two weeks. That was too long.

The sound of a popular radio show echoed through the small bungalow. I walked through the house to my mother's bedroom and found her in bed lying against her pillows, listening to *Woman's Hour* on her favorite local station, WCCO.

"Hello, Mamma," I said tenderly and leaned over to kiss her cheek. "How are you feeling today?"

"Charlotte," she said in a weakened voice, "turn off the radio so we can talk."

I switched the Somerset radio off and gingerly sat on the edge of the bed. She looked more fatigued and fragile since the last time I'd been with her and it worried me. Her sky-blue eyes were underscored with dark circles, as though she hadn't been sleeping well. Her once beautiful flaxen hair, now gray, hung listlessly about her shoulders. "How are you feeling?" I repeated.

"About the same." She clasped her bony fingers around mine. "Some days are better than others. I'm a little tired today. How are you?" She touched my abdomen. "And the little one…"

"The baby is fine, Mamma. My energy is back and I rarely get sick anymore."

"I worry about you, honey." The lines in her pale face were etched with sadness and an expression of helplessness that made my heart ache. "You should never have left Gus. He took good care of you. He takes good care of all of us."

"It's become too dangerous to stay with him. Besides, I'm doing fine." I patted her hand, upset that with all the problems she had, she worried about me more than herself. "I found a job. I'm working as a housekeeper in a big house across town."

"A housekeeper?" She looked horrified. "That's such hard work."

Footsteps running across the upper floor disrupted the conversation. My younger sister, Mary Frances, occupied a small bedroom upstairs. "Mamma, who's here?"

I rose from the bed and walked to the bottom of the stairway. Looking up, I smiled. "Guess who?"

My fourteen-year-old sister let out a loud shriek. "Char!" She flew down the stairs and into my arms, squealing with delight. We hugged quickly then she pulled away, bubbling with laughter. "I'm so glad you're here! Are you staying overnight?" She pulled on her flaxen braids with an excited gasp. "Will you cut my hair? I want it to look just like yours. Please? Oh, please, Char?" Her bright blue eyes, large and fringed with delicate pale lashes searched mine. "Mamma says I'm too young to wear my hair in a bob, but she'll listen to you if you say it's okay."

"Mary Frances," Mamma said sternly from the bedroom. Her illness hadn't affected her hearing. It was as sharp as ever. "I said no haircut until you're sixteen and that's final!"

I folded my arms. "Sounds like Mamma's putting her foot down this time, Francie." I always called her the nickname she'd had since birth.

Protruding her bottom lip in an exaggerated pout, Francie followed me back into the bedroom and plopped on the bed. I pulled up a chair.

"Has Gus been around?" I hated to ask, but I needed to know.

Francie's head bobbed. "Uh-huh. He was here yesterday and he asked about you again."

My chest tightened. "Please don't tell him you've seen me."

"We won't." Francie leaned back on her hands. "He thinks because we're family, we're obligated to let him know if you contact us, but we'd never do that."

"That's why I'm not telling you where I'm living now. So, you don't have to lie when he asks again." I stared at Mamma. "Gus doesn't take kindly to people who don't tell him the truth."

Though I didn't believe Gus would retaliate against my family for keeping my whereabouts a secret, he *would* find a way to trick the truth out of them. When he did, he'd come after me. I had no idea what he'd do when he found me, but I was determined to never find out. If it weren't for my mother and sister, I'd be long gone, but they were the only family I had. I couldn't leave Francie and I would never abandon Mamma.

"I want you to have this." Opening my handbag, I pulled out ten dollars of my first week's wages and offered the bills to Mamma. "I'll help you as much as I can."

She pushed my hand away. "No, please keep it for yourself."

"But—"

"Gus gives us money every time he comes around," Francie blurted. "He just gave Mamma five hundred dollars yesterday."

Mamma reached inside her pillowcase and pulled out a rolled wad of bills secured with a rubber band. "Take this. You need it more than we do."

I stared in horror at the money. "No, Mamma, I can't do that. It's not right—"

Francie waved her hand in a dismissive gesture. "You don't need to worry. Gus said there was more where that came from."

Trying to buy their loyalty, I thought nervously. *I know he wants to be good to them, but he never does anything for free...*

Francie took the money and placed it in my hand. "This isn't all of it. We kept some for groceries and the light bill, but we want you to have some, too." She glanced at Mamma then back at me. "Besides, if Papa comes home and finds it, he'll take it."

If Gus found out about that...

My fingers closed over the roll. "Okay, I'll keep it safe for you, but I'm *not* going to spend it."

"It's for the baby," Mamma insisted. "You need to find a place to live. Charlotte, I worry so much—" Before she could finish, she began to cough violently. It ended the discussion but opened up a new set of worries for me.

Francie and I managed to calm her down and went into the kitchen to make her favorite beverage, Earl Grey tea with lemon and honey. "How is Mamma's heart?" I whispered as I filled the tea kettle with water. "She looks weaker than the last time I was here."

Francie shrugged, but her eyes reflected a sadness beyond her years. "About the same. Gus still sends a nurse to check on her three times a week and he says we need to get a phone so I can call the nurse if Mamma takes a turn for the worse."

"That's a good idea. Then I can call and find out how she's doing, too." The moment the words left my lips I realized it would never happen. The phone would be on a party line with the neighbors listening in. One of them might somehow inform Gus...

Francie made the tea while I started dinner. We ate together in Mamma's bedroom, serving Mamma's food on a bed tray and setting a small table for Francie and me. After dinner, Mamma fell asleep. I helped

Francie clean up the kitchen before I took my leave.

"Oh! I almost forgot," Francie said as I stopped with my hand on the screen door. I'd already donned my glasses and scrunched my hat low on my head. "Wait a minute. I need to show you something."

Stifling a yawn, I waited impatiently as Francie bolted upstairs to her bedroom. The sun dipped low in the sky and I was anxious to catch the streetcar. The long, emotional day was beginning to take a toll on me.

Francie returned a minute later with a folded newspaper in her hand. She held it out for me to read. "Have you seen this?"

The headline read *Federal agents raid La Coquette.*

"No," I said as I spotted the date—a couple of days after the incident. Back then, I was too sick to do anything except sleep and puke. "Where did you get it?"

She handed it to me. "Mr. Olson, our new neighbor down the block, came to visit Mamma last week and he brought her a stack of newspapers to read. I thought you might want to know what it says about the raid and everything."

"Sure." My voice sounded very *unsure* as I accepted the newspaper. Did I really want to relive that horrible day again? No, but I did need to know if the paper had uncovered any new facts about me. I tucked it under my arm. "I'll read it tonight when I get home."

I tugged on Francie's braid and kissed her goodbye, leaving before she could see the tears threatening to spill from my eyes. Hustling down the alley with my head lowered and my gaze fixed straight ahead, questions spun in my mind. How did my life turn into such a mess? Why did Mamma have to be worse every time I saw her? What would I do if anything hap—when the inevitable day came?

Mixed in with my thoughts was the heart-pounding fear I would one day run into my husband again and be forced to confront him. Given the circumstances with Mamma, it was highly possible. Would he be understanding or would he unleash his anger on me? Gus was a powerful man with a massive empire, but he hadn't built it by forgiving people. The question plaguing me the most was, what would I do? Would I run away or stand and fight for my baby's future safety and happiness?

A sob escaped my throat. I had no idea.

*　　*　　*

Early the next morning, before sunrise, I awoke to the sound of birds chirping outside my window. Golden light from the small lamp on my dresser illuminated the room. The newspaper lay next to me on the bed, unread. I must have fallen asleep as soon as my head hit the pillow and hadn't moved all night long.

"I have to get up," I murmured with a groan as I buried my face in the pillow. Unfortunately, my body didn't agree. The next thing I knew, I awoke again to a room filled with sunlight. "Oh, my gosh," I cried as I stumbled out of bed and grabbed a clean uniform. The newspaper slid off the bed and landed on the floor. "I'm late!"

In record time, I dressed, straightened my room, washed my face, and ran down to the kitchen to get the morning coffee brewing. I managed to get breakfast ready by seven, but through the morning I battled fatigue as I struggled to concentrate on my duties.

Mr. Van Elsberg left the house right after breakfast and didn't return until late that evening. His absence gave Miss Amundsen all day to check on my work and find fault with nearly everything I did. Tired and grumpy as I was, I held my tongue, though it took extreme self-control on my part to put up with her carping.

Daniel made himself scarce for most of the day, busily sanding down the front porch to apply a fresh coat of paint. I made him a hot lunch and took it out to him to get a bit of fresh air.

Miss Amundsen left promptly at five o'clock. The moment she stepped onto the front sidewalk, I took off my apron and headed up to my room for the rest of the evening. Collapsing on my bed, I closed my eyes and slept for a while. It was dark by the time I awoke and turned on my lamp. The newspaper lay folded under my pillow. Curious, I pulled it out. The first two sentences caught my eye...

On the evening of May 15th, Gus "Lucky" LeDoux, the king of Minnesota bootleggers escaped from his luxurious castle when Federal agents raided La Coquette and shut it down for good. Will his kingdom of moonshiners be next?

All of the money Gus had paid in bribes to local officials to look the other way failed to do him any good once the Federal Government decided to go after him.

Anxious to find out if I could learn something new, I quickly skimmed the page. The article stated that Gus and his men had shot and killed several Prohibition agents before slipping from the grasp of Federal law enforcement, but I'd learned that weeks ago. It also stated that La Coquette had suffered major damage to the interior of the building when the crowd stampeded the exits, trying to escape. I knew that, too, but not much else in connection with the business except that Federal agents had broken open all the barrels of Gus' private reserve of whiskey and drained them dry.

That wouldn't stop Gus. The Feds had merely slowed him down for a few days. There was a lot more good quality liquor where that came from and Gus had probably set up shop somewhere else by now anyway. He surrounded himself with skilled people and his network of "moonshiners" in Stearns and Morrison Counties was extremely loyal. It would take more than one run-in with the Feds to destroy what he'd spent years building.

I continued reading the rest of the article and...

What?

I sat up, fully awake now.

Mr. LeDoux escaped from the authorities unharmed however, his wife may have encountered a tragic fate. Local residents living behind LeDoux's auto dealership told of a woman fitting Charlotte LeDoux's description being dragged against her will by Albert Schultz. Mr. Schultz, a former bodyguard of Gus LeDoux, shot and killed a federal agent then forced Mrs. LeDoux into a car and led authorities on a chase to Swede Hollow where his vehicle drove into Phalen Creek after he was shot and killed behind the wheel.

Mrs. LeDoux's body was not found at the scene, but the agents in pursuit discovered blood on the passenger seat and several personal items affirmed belonging to her. Residents in Swede Hollow claimed no one saw her that night and others speculated she may have been wounded, fallen into the creek while trying to escape, drowned, and swept away by the current. Anyone who has seen Mrs. LeDoux or knows of her whereabouts should contact the Bureau of Investigation.

Laying back on the bed, I stared up at the ceiling, dazed. On one hand, the current theory of my supposed death couldn't have been farther from the truth. On the other hand…the current theory of my supposed death meant that no one was expecting to find me anywhere but at the bottom of Phalen Creek. Everyone thought I was *dead*. I wondered if Gus believed it as well.

I fell asleep thinking about the car crashing into the creek and dreamed I was back at the scene, desperately trying to wade through the water. The Feds had caught up with me and were jumping out of their vehicles. I tried to get away, but the harder I struggled, the deeper the water became until it reached my neck. The sound of slamming car doors and loud voices frightened me. I started screaming for Gus…

* * *

I awoke with a gasp, fighting to catch my breath, the dream still fresh in my mind. The background noises and those people—everything had sounded so real. Suddenly, a door slammed downstairs and the clamor of excited voices echoed through the house. I lay still, my heart pounding as I listened intently.

"Hey, Will," a man's deep voice hollered, "where do you keep the hooch?"

Wondering how many people had arrived, I rose from the bed, straightened my clothes, and went down to the kitchen. I found Mr. Van Elsberg looking through the cabinets. "Oh, there you are. Where do you keep the fancy whiskey glasses?"

"I'll get them." I went into the dining room to retrieve the crystal "lowball" glasses I'd seen in the china closet. In the living room, directly across from where I stood, were two women and a man. The man sat on the davenport wearing a brown pinstripe suit and smoking a cigarette. His light brown hair parted down the middle, round, wire-rimmed glasses and pencil-thin mustache gave him a polished, professional image. He didn't strike me as another investigator and I wondered what he did for a living.

The women, one blonde and one brunette stood in front of the Victor credenza, looking at records to play on the Victrola. I recognized one of them—Mr. Van Elsberg's sister, Madeline. The woman who thought she'd seen me somewhere else…

As quickly as I could, I quietly retrieved the glasses and slipped back into the kitchen. "Will you be needing anything else tonight?" I had my fingers crossed, hoping Mr. Van Elsberg would say no.

"Make something for us to snack on," he declared as he took two glasses in each hand.

Make *something*? I had no idea what he meant by that. "What kind of snack would you like?"

"I like everything." He turned and walked out of the kitchen, leaving me to stare after him in bewilderment.

I went into the pantry, looking for inspiration. On a top shelf, I saw several cans of Underwood Deviled Ham. Right away I knew he must have purchased them to make sandwiches when he was in between domestic servants. Stacking them on a top shelf was a dead giveaway! A woman would not have stored them so high, whereas they were easily reachable for a man with long arms. I dragged a chair over to the pantry and retrieved the little cans as I mulled over a makeshift recipe for an appetizer in my head.

"Minced onion, mustard, mayonnaise, a pinch of black pepper," I murmured as I pulled open the Frigidaire and pulled out the first two ingredients. A jar of sweet pickles caught my eye. *Hmmm...* I thought and grabbed the pickle jar as well. *And maybe some cheese. Wait—I don't have any crackers...*

The women were dancing to a song playing on the Victrola. The men were relaxing on the davenport with their whiskey glasses. A chorus of cheers greeted me as I delivered the food.

The song playing on the Victrola ended. Madeline lifted the tonearm and moved it aside then turned her attention to the food.

Mr. Van Elsberg took the small stack of plates from me. "Here you go, Gloria," he said, handing a plate to his date for the evening, the tall blonde wearing a black sequined dress. "Help yourself." Then he gave one to his sister and her date, an attorney named Peter Garrett.

"Scoot over, Peter," Gloria said as she wedged herself in between the men and snuggled up to Mr. Van Elsberg. "I'm hungry and these little open-faced sandwiches look good!" She snatched one and began to nibble on it. "No, they're excellent!" She looked up at me. "If you ever get tired of working for Will, come and talk to *me*. My family is always looking for a good cook."

Though she meant it to be a compliment, my cheeks inflamed with discomfort. "Will that be all?" I asked politely, but at the same time, my stomach churned with anxiety. I didn't want praise or the offer of a new job; I just wanted to retreat to the kitchen.

"Your *voice* is so familiar," Madeline remarked and shook her head in puzzlement. "I just wish I could remember where I've heard it before." She glanced at her date for the evening. "Peter, where have we heard that voice?"

Peter merely shrugged as he stuffed his mouth with ham salad on toast.

My heart jumped to my throat. "I—I probably sound like someone else you've met."

Her dark brows knitted together. "Have you ever been to La Coquette?"

My knees started to shake. "No," I said as I placed my hand upon a parlor table for support. "Never." I glanced at Mr. Van Elsberg and caught him frowning at my reaction. I removed my hand from the table and stood up straight. "Will you need anything else tonight?"

"No, that will be all, Esther, but be sure to clean this room tomorrow first thing."

I caught his meaning and promised I would. I didn't want Miss Amundsen to see any trace of the evening's activities and jealously grill me about it any more than he did. At his nod, I retreated to the kitchen as fast as my legs could carry me and collapsed on the stairway, leaning my head against the wall. Miss Madeline's curiosity and persistent questioning frightened me. What if she figured out who I really was?

I couldn't stay here much longer. It was too risky. Trouble was, I didn't want to leave...

Chapter Five

For the next several weeks, I worked hard at my job and slowly settled into a routine. I made a list of weekly chores and constantly updated it, spreading them out over six days so I had light chores on Sunday. Mr. Van Elsberg gave me advance notice of when he'd be bringing company home at night—usually on Saturday—and the number of guests so I could plan accordingly. On Friday afternoons, I'd slip out the back door the same time Miss Amundsen walked out the front door and headed for the market to get the items I needed for lobster or crab canapés, deviled eggs, and other assorted appetizers. During the week, I experimented with easy desserts that I could make ahead of time, such as a crème velvet cake with pineapple frosting or gingerbread slices topped with whipped cream. The party preparations were an enjoyable diversion from my daily routine and I always set aside a single serving of the food to provide a treat for Daniel. The grocery bill notably increased, but Mr. Van Elsberg never said a word to me about cutting back on the amounts or making less expensive dishes.

One Friday morning in mid-July, I stood at the kitchen sink peeling potatoes when I heard the thumping of weighty footsteps crossing the front porch. Curious, I paused, holding a half-peeled potato as I listened for the *b r-r-r-ing* of the doorbell. But none came. Instead, a heavy hand pounded insistently on the door. Mr. Van Elsberg had just donned a suit jacket to go out for the day and had reached for his Panama hat. He froze, his hand holding the hat suspended in mid-air.

"Will, there's a stranger at the door," Miss Amundsen announced as she peered through the parlor window. A thread of uncertainty in her voice caused me to slow down at the kitchen door and wait for his reply before proceeding. She walked toward the foyer. "I don't recognize him so he's not one of our current clients. Did you forget to tell me you made an appointment today?"

"No," he said, checking his watch. "I have no idea who it is. I should be leaving right now."

He stood between me and the front door so I couldn't see the caller, but I didn't move. The wariness in Miss Amundsen's behavior made me cautious. I watched as Mr. Van Elsberg placed his hat back on the hat rack, opened the interior door, and stepped toward the screen door. He opened it slowly. "May I help you?"

"Are you Will Van Elsberg? I'm here to retain your services."

I nearly fainted. Clutching the doorframe for support, I fell back against the kitchen wall, my heart pounding like a sledgehammer in my chest. I barely heard the door open and two sets of footsteps walk into the front parlor, but I didn't need to because I recognized the sound and the tempo of both. One set of footsteps belonged to my boss.

The other belonged to my husband.

Dear God, my thoughts screamed, *how did he find me?* I nearly bolted for the back door until I realized something important. Gus would have come right to the point if he'd known I was hiding from him in this very house and he wouldn't have been polite about it. He wouldn't have bothered to knock, either. Still, it didn't comfort me much to know he stood in the next room. Would he recognize me if he saw me wearing an oversized maid uniform with red henna hair and wire-rimmed eyeglasses? I didn't want to find out.

Gus introduced himself and said his lawyer, Harv Katzenbaum, had recommended Mr. Van Elsberg. My boss replied that he'd handled the investigations of a few cases for Harv.

"Have a seat, Mr. LeDoux. Miss Amundsen, please bring Mr. LeDoux some coffee."

Miss Amundsen charged into the kitchen. "What are you doing standing around? Coffee for the client. *Now.*"

I had a choice; slip out the back door and never come back, or scrunch my headband down on my forehead and quickly serve the coffee without looking at anyone. I was considering exercising the first option as soon as I had poured the coffee into a mug and arranged it on a tray with cream and sugar containers.

"Esther!"

Making the choice for me, Miss Amundsen grabbed my arm and jolted me into action, marching me into the front parlor. Keeping my head down, I set the tray on the parlor table, pulled away from her, and hustled back to the kitchen to beat the band.

"I don't know what's gotten into her," Miss Amundsen snapped at my retreating form. "Mr. LeDoux, would you care for cream or sugar in your coffee?"

"Ah, no thank you, Miss," Gus said. "I'll just drink it black."

The tall sliding doors of thick oak on two sides of the front parlor were often used to shutter the room from the rest of the house when Mr. Van Elsberg had appointments with clients. Once Miss Amundsen pulled the heavy doors together, I cautiously stepped into the dining room and peered through the living room. The parlor doors were closed to both the living room and the foyer, but one set didn't quite fit together anymore. Desperate to eavesdrop on the conversation, I quietly tiptoed into the living room and peered through the sliver of space between them.

"I want to hire you to find my wife," Gus said, getting right to the point. He pulled a large white envelope filled with cash from the inside pocket of his suit jacket and placed it on the desk with a heavy thump. Gus always had a lot of money on hand and preferred to deal with most things that way. Cash never left a trail of any kind and enough of it could buy just about anything he wanted or needed.

He produced a flask of whiskey from an outside pocket and unscrewed the top. "I don't know if she's alive or dead, but she's been gone for almost two months." He poured a long shot of the whiskey into his coffee. "I've lost a lot of sleep over this." His hands tremored slightly as he replaced the cap on his flask and buried it back inside his coat pocket. "I need closure, Will, one way or the other."

Gus was extremely tall with wide shoulders, long arms, and a barrel chest. He always wore expensive, hand-tailored suits and kept his thick, sandy hair neatly trimmed, but today he resembled a mere shadow of his former self. The days-old stubble along his jaw gave him a haggard look for a man in his mid-thirties. His sage eyes were bloodshot from heavy drinking, the lids drooping from exhaustion and extreme duress. For a moment, I almost felt sorry for him, but at the same time, I glanced through the window and saw one of Gus' many vehicles, a Packard Phaeton, parked alongside the curb. Adrienne Devereaux sat in the back seat, peering through the open window toward the house. An icy band surrounded my heart.

What a slap in the face! He's hiring a private detective to find his wife while his mistress waits for him in the car.

Mr. Van Elsberg sat at his desk, calmly assessing the situation. "I've read about your wife's disappearance and I'm sorry for your loss. I'll take this case and provide you with an answer, but before I begin, I want you to understand that you need to prepare yourself for the possibility she may be dead."

Gus replied with a solemn nod and a gulp of his spiked coffee.

Mr. Van Elsberg opened a desk drawer and pulled out a legal pad to write on. "I'll need an address or a phone number to contact you. Do you have a photograph of her?"

"Yeah, I've got one." Gus set down his coffee and pulled out his wallet, thumbing through it. "I never give out personal information, but I'll you give the phone number of where I'm temporarily staying." He looked up. "I don't want you passing it along to anyone else, understand? Whatever information we exchange in this room stays *here*."

"Of course," Mr. Van Elsberg said evenly. "You can trust both me and my secretary to keep anything you say in the strictest confidence."

Gus found what he wanted and placed the small, tattered photo on the desk next to the cash envelope. "Here, this is our wedding picture. She's pretty young there, but she hasn't changed much."

Mr. Van Elsberg picked up the photo and stared at it, frowning. "Tell me everything you remember about the last time you saw her."

Gus glanced keenly out the large front window, obviously watching for any unusual movement on the street. "It was the night La Coquette went down. I sent her to Swede Hollow with Al Schultz. She didn't want to go with him, but I thought she'd be safer without me." He stared at Mr. Van Elsberg, his jaw clenching. "I never thought I'd lose either one of them, much less both."

"Are you sure she wasn't apprehended by Federal agents?"

"Yeah," Gus replied emphatically. "There's only one way in and out of the hollow, so I couldn't approach the area until the Feds finished their investigation. The car was still in the water when I got there, but by that time, Al's body had been taken away. I talked to the residents. No one living there saw Char at all that night, but I know she'd been there because they said she'd left behind her hat. Pieces of her necklace were scattered all over the vehicle and there was blood on the seat. Some people thought she may have been wounded. After the car crashed, if she'd tried to get out, it's possible she fainted or lost her balance and fell into the creek then got swept away with the current."

Miss Amundsen sat at her desk, her chair turned toward the men as she held a pen and stenographer's notebook in her hands, jotting down the facts in shorthand.

Mr. Van Elsberg sat very still at his desk, listening intently. "What was she wearing?"

"Ah…" Gus gulped his coffee. "All I remember," he said slowly as he flicked another glance at the activity out on the street, "is she had on this…this silvery thing. It was short and fit her like a second skin, but I can't tell you much more than that."

Yeah, but I'll bet you could describe every nip and tuck of Adrienne's silk undergarments, I thought angrily. I wanted to scream out loud that the reason he couldn't remember what I had on that night was because he'd been too preoccupied with his mistress to notice me—

"It seems to me," Mr. Van Elsberg said, interrupting my internal diatribe, "if your wife did drown, her body would have washed up somewhere by now. And that dress you've described would have been hard to miss." He tapped a pencil on his desk blotter, thinking. "Why did you send her to Swede Hollow?"

"It was the safest place for her to be. She grew up there. She was living in the hollow when I first met her. Her father worked at my family's brewery." Gus drained his coffee. "She was only fifteen at the time and so innocent. The prettiest girl I'd ever seen."

"Does she have any family living there?"

"No." Gus shook his head. "Char's mother is alive, but she's an invalid. Her father is still living, too." He snorted. "Floyd's a drunk and the only reason he comes around to see his wife is to confiscate whatever he can get his hands on to buy more *moon*."

"If your wife knew people in the hollow well enough to trust them, is it possible someone there may have helped her get away?"

"Sure, there are plenty of people who would help her if she asked them." Gus folded his arms, his voice rising. "I keep thinking about it—and wondering if someone lied to me about not knowing her whereabouts. If that's true and I ever found out…"

Mr. Van Elsberg stared hard at Gus; his dark brows furrowed with interest at this unexpected turn in the conversation. "Why do you think a person would do that? Help her escape and conceal it from you?"

A car zoomed by the house. Gus jumped to his feet and warily peered out the window. "I don't know, but I've got my suspicions."

Mr. Van Elsberg continued to remain calm as Gus began pacing the floor. If he found Gus' escalating agitation unsettling, he didn't show it. He didn't show any emotion. "What are your suspicions?"

Gus stopped. "Someone I've known for a long time—a woman—told me that Char claimed she was in the family way."

Miss Amundsen stopped writing.

Mr. Van Elsberg dropped his pencil. "Are you saying that your wife was going to have a baby but you didn't know about it?"

Gus shrugged in frustration. "Look, it isn't as if we haven't tried. Char's been wanting to have a baby ever since we got married, but she keeps losing them in the early months. I didn't believe Sally at first, but she's not the kind of woman who gossips." He pulled out his flask again and unscrewed the cap. "Maybe Char blames me." He took a long swallow. "Maybe she thought that if she tried to have a child with someone else…"

My stomach nervously flip-flopped. *So, he knows about the baby…* Then another thought crossed my mind, making me bristle. *How dare he suggest that someone else is the father! When did he stop trusting his own wife? When he'd started being untrustworthy himself?*

I didn't blame Sally Wentworth for telling him the truth. Knowing what a big heart she had for me and Gus, it was just the thing she would do if she thought I was in danger. I missed her terribly, but given the situation, our paths would probably never cross again.

A splinter of doubt began to plague my heart. Was I wrong to deny Gus the right to know his child? Was I wrong—no, terribly selfish—to deny my child the right to know his father?

Mr. Van Elsberg picked up his pencil again and repositioned his legal pad. "Who were your wife's closest friends at the club? What about employees she interacted with every day? Let's start there. Give me a list."

Gus began reciting the names of women he knew I associated with on an ongoing basis. Then he made a verbal list of the women we had employed, both at the club and our home.

Mr. Van Elsberg looked up. "What about male associates? Who did she regularly socialize with at the club?"

Gus' mouth formed a deep scowl as he shoved his hands into his pockets. "There were a few regulars who tried to get friendly with Char. I put most of them in their places right away, but I didn't watch my wife every minute, so she could have had an affair with someone I don't know about." He looked straight at Mr. Van Elsberg. "So, you think she might have taken up with some fella in the club and faked her death to leave town with him?"

"I don't know." Mr. Van Elsberg stared at his notes and rubbed his chin. I could tell he was trying to tread carefully through such an emotional issue. "At this point, I'm simply suggesting we consider every possibility."

Instead of agreeing, Gus went deathly still, his eyes blazing. "If I find she's double-crossed me with another guy and I locate where they're staying, *I'll kill him.*" He slammed his fist on the desk so hard the windows rattled. "I'll kill both of them!"

My hand flew over my mouth to stifle a gasp as I reflexively backed away from the door. Miss Amundsen shrieked and leaped from her chair, her pad and pencil crashing to the floor. Mr. Van Elsberg jumped up and swiftly rounded the desk confronting Gus nose to nose. "Easy, LeDoux," he said in a steely voice, "I know you're upset, but you're frightening my secretary. I need you to *calm down*."

Mr. Van Elsberg turned to Miss Amundsen gently placing his hands upon her shoulders. It was the first time I'd ever seen him even get close enough to her to touch her. "Take a deep breath, Louisa. That's good. Now go into the kitchen and get yourself a cool glass of water. Then I want you to take the rest of the day off. All right? And tell Esther she has the afternoon off, too."

I stumbled back to the kitchen, hoping to disappear before Miss Amundsen came out of the parlor and caught me running away. I'd barely reached the back stairway when I heard the double parlor doors slide open. Clinging to the railing, I struggled to stand up straight, but my stomach ached from twisting into a tight knot of fear.

Oh, dear God. If Gus finds out who I am, he'll kill us all.

It was now or never. I needed to get as far away from this house as possible. By taking this job, I'd unknowingly risked the lives of not only my baby but everyone else in this residence as well. If Gus discovered I'd been hiding in plain sight and showed up for retribution on a night when Mr. Van Elsberg had guests…

"More coffee!" Miss Amundsen stood behind me, literally shouting.

Unable to straighten, I turned my head instead, glaring at her over my shoulder. Gus' outburst had frightened her so much, her lashes were wet. What little color resided in her pale complexion had turned ashen. At this point, however, I didn't care. Her yapping only added to my agitation. "What?"

"I *said*, get Mr. LeDoux another cup of coffee. *Now.*"

Not a word about taking the afternoon off.

"I can't," I shot back, wincing with pain. "I'm not feeling well."

"Is that so? There wasn't anything wrong with you when you were spying on us through the crack in the door."

I nearly swallowed my tongue. *How did she know?* "I can't," I repeated.

"You can't?" she parroted in a mocking tone. Her eyes narrowed. "Or you *won't?*"

I'd had enough of her imperious attitude today. "Take your pick. I don't really care," I murmured.

Her face suddenly took on a triumphant sneer. "That insolent remark just got you fired. After you serve the coffee, get your things packed, and *get out.*"

The back door opened and Daniel burst into the kitchen. "Is everything all right in here? I thought I heard someone scream."

"It's nothing to concern yourself over," Miss Amundsen snapped. "Get back to work."

With a silent glare, he turned around and walked out the back door.

She turned to me and snapped her fingers. "And as for you, if you want to get paid, get busy and serve that coffee!"

"Serve it yourself." I turned and practically crawled up the stairs. Once I reached my room, I slowly lowered myself on the bed and rested. My body began to relax immediately and the pain eased up. It didn't do much to lessen the pain in my heart, though.

From the moment I'd heard Gus' footsteps in the foyer, I'd known my time here was up, no matter how much I wanted to stay. *Better sooner than later*, I thought, trying to see the practical side of the situation. I only had a month or two anyway before my tummy started to become round enough to notice. Then I would be dismissed if I hadn't already left on my own. Still, I couldn't shake the sadness welling up inside of me. Other than my issues with Miss Amundsen, I'd found peace and contentment here, like I'd experienced growing up in Swede Hollow.

Forcing myself to get up, I took off my uniform and stockings and slipped into a new two-piece frock I'd purchased last Wednesday afternoon before I went to visit Mamma. The green circular skirt and matching tunic-style blouse had a flat collar edged in a narrow braid. It felt good to get that hot, sweaty uniform off and put on something more comfortable. I scrunched my hat on my head and threw the few items I possessed into my satchel, including my handbag—and the revolver with the pearl handle. I'd always detested that thing, but I feared Gus would find out if I tried to trade it for money at a hock shop.

The front door banged shut, rattling my windows. Stepping to the window, I peered down at the street and watched as Gus strode down the sidewalk. A bodyguard followed him like a bloodhound. Holding a submachine gun in one hand, the man opened the back door for Gus with his other hand, all the while searching the immediate area for any signs of trouble.

I waited until the car drove away then headed for the servants' stairs and left the house by the back door. I walked down the alley with tears clouding my eyes as I wondered what to do now. Honestly, I had no idea.

All I knew was I had to keep going.

Chapter Six

The happy lunchtime crowd at Big Louie's Soda Shop filled all of the tables and booths. Luckily for me, a couple who had finished their lunch saw me looking for a place to sit and decided to take their leave so I could have their booth. After thanking them, I placed my satchel on the floor under the table, slid in, and sat staring at the dirty dishes on the tabletop, numbed by the events of the day. The people around me talked and laughed as they enjoyed their lunch, but their clamor made little sense to me. The events of the day had left me so exhausted I could barely move.

A young, freckle-faced waitress appeared immediately with a tray to clear away the empty glasses and plates and wipe down the table. She smiled. "Do you need a minute to look over the menu?"

Realizing I hadn't even thought about what I wanted to eat, I slowly pulled out the paper menu sandwiched between the sugar and napkin dispensers. "Yes, thank you."

Dropping her towel on the table, she wiped it clean with a quick, swirling motion then pointed to a chalkboard hanging on the wall. "The daily specials are on the board. Just lay down your menu when you're ready to order."

I nodded and pretended to look it over after she left, but my mind reeled so hard with unanswered questions I could barely concentrate. Where would I go? What type of employment would I pursue next? Without a job, I couldn't afford to eat here now, and to make things worse, I'd left today without getting my week's wages. I knew I should leave, but I was hungry. Who could look for a job on an empty stomach? I rationalized that I'd use the opportunity to boost my morale with a hot lunch and a cold sundae before considering my next move.

"Are you finished with the newspaper?" I asked the white-haired man at the table across from me.

He picked up the folded *St. Paul Pioneer Press* next to his empty plate and handed it to me. "Help yourself."

"Thank you." I planned to scour the "Help Wanted" ads for a new job while I ate my lunch.

I'm so tired. I should go home and spend the night with Mamma before I start looking again. I miss her and I always get a good night's sleep there. The trouble is, though, I don't want her to worry about me or my problems. She's got enough to deal with...

If not today, I would have to visit them soon. She and Francie might need some of the money they'd given me. I was *not* going to spend it on myself. I could work for a living. They couldn't and if anything happened to Gus, the money would stop coming, leaving them in dire straits.

Having decided on my lunch, I set down my menu and waited for the waitress to take my order.

"What would you like?" she asked once she reappeared at the table.

"I'll take the egg salad sandwich special with beef soup," I replied. "Just water to drink." I needed to save my beverage money for ice cream instead.

After she left again, I stared at the folded paper and realized it was time to quit feeling sorry for myself. My problems weren't going to magically solve themselves nor were they going to get any easier by procrastinating. I flipped open the paper to the "Help Wanted" section and was busy skimming the ads when someone appeared at my table. I assumed it was my waitress, informing me they were already out of the daily special. Looking up, however, I found myself staring into the eyes of Daniel Blythe. He stood clutching his hat in his hands, his green eyes reflecting great concern. "Hey, lady, do you mind if a fella invites himself to join you?"

"Help yourself," I said, using the same response I'd just received from the man who'd given me his newspaper. "You're looking pretty grim. What's wrong?"

He slid into the booth and laid his tan newsboy-style hat by his side on the seat. Anxiety radiated off him like heat waves from a robust fire. He glanced at the newspaper spread across the table and saw which section I was reading. Reaching out, he placed his splayed hand over the paper and looked into my eyes. "Don't go, Esther."

"I'm sorry, Daniel," I said quietly. "I have to find another job."

"You're the best housekeeper and cook we've ever had since I started working there. Mr. Van Elsberg and I like you. We *need* you. Come back."

"I can't. Miss Amundsen fired me for refusing to carry out an order." I shrugged. "And for telling her *where to go* when she reprimanded me…"

The young waitress approached our table and smiled at my dining companion. "Would you like to order?"

"No thank you," he said politely. "I'm not going to be here long." When she left, he turned his attention back to me. "*She* can't fire you. She's overstepped her authority. When *he* found out what she'd done, he blew his temper."

"Mr. Van Elsberg got angry?" That bit of information surprised the living daylights out of me. I'd never seen him get angry with her. Miss Amundsen raised her voice to him whenever she complained about me, but he'd always remained extremely patient with her. "How do you know this?"

"They were in the kitchen arguing when I came up the back steps. I didn't want to intrude, so I waited until they'd finished and left the room before I came into the house, but what I heard nearly curled my ears."

Instead of leaving immediately as she had been instructed, Miss Amundsen must have waited around until Gus left to give Mr. Van Elsberg the good news of my departure...or so she thought. I rested my chin on the heel of my hand. "Wh-what happened?"

"He yelled at her—that's what he did," Daniel said seriously. "Out and out hollered at the top of his lungs. Told her he'd never given her permission to hire or fire anybody and from now on she should stick to the job he'd hired her to do or she'd be the next one out the door."

My jaw dropped. Mr. Van Elsberg had instructed me to come to him if I had any problems, but after what happened today, I didn't think it mattered anymore. Besides, I wasn't a troublemaker.

Daniel reached across the table and took my hand. "After she left in a huff, slamming the front door, I went to Mr. Van Elsberg and told him I'd heard everything. I asked him if he'd take you back if I could locate you. He was greatly troubled about your leaving and said he was going to drive around and see if he could find you himself." Daniel squeezed my hand. "I came straight here, hoping you'd stopped for one last ice cream sundae before you disappeared completely."

I didn't know what to say. Though I could clearly tell he was happy and relieved he'd found me, his eyes mirrored sadness over my departure. His deep voice trembled with despair. He wanted in the worst way to convince me to come back to work.

"It's time I moved on, Daniel," I said candidly. "There are things about me…" I took a deep breath. "If you knew what I've done, you'd understand why it's impossible to go back."

"Look," he said and covered both of his hands over mine. "Whatever it is, I'll help you work through it." He paused, his thick, rust-colored brows deepening. "Did you steal something from the house? Money? Liquor?"

If only it was that simple! I shook my head. "No, nothing like that."

"Then what's wrong?"

"I can't talk about it."

He glanced around to make sure no one was listening to our conversation then leaned forward. "I'm sorry, Esther," he said softly. "I don't mean to pry, but I can see how painful it is for you. Whatever it is, you can't change the past so let it go. It's time to start over."

Oh, how desperately I wished that was true!

His belief in me and a genuine desire to help me brought tears to my eyes. Friendship like this was worth its weight in gold, but I couldn't drag him into my situation and risk his life. Or anyone else who might try to help me. Tears of frustration slid down my cheeks.

"I want to help you, Esther. Please don't shut me out." My tears seemed to spur him on. "Tell me why you're so afraid."

"Why should I trust you?" I asked angrily, wiping my cheeks with the backs of my hands. "Why should I trust any man?"

"You've always been good to me, Esther. I want to repay your kindness," he said earnestly. "That's what friends are for."

He spoke the words with such compassion I knew he was sincere. His honesty touched my heart yet it saddened me, too, because there was nothing he *could* do to change my situation. On the other hand, the best thing I could do for him was simply walk away and forget we ever met.

I decided to tell him part of the truth about me—but only the part that would drop me so low in his eyes it would end our friendship. Then we would go our separate ways. I looked at him point-blank. "I'm going to have a baby."

His face blanched. His eyes widened with shock.

It bothered me greatly to deceive him by letting him think I was a single woman having an illegitimate child, but if it achieved my purpose, so be it.

After a moment, he said, "The man responsible for…for your predicament—is he going to take care of you?"

I shook my head. "It's up to me to take care of myself." I held up the newspaper. "There is an entire column of housekeeping jobs in this paper. If I got a better paying job, I could save more money to live on when I'm so far along I have to quit working."

He glanced at the newspaper in my hand. "With your personality, I have no doubt you could get another job right away. Staying healthy in your condition while doing that job is another matter."

"What do you mean?"

He folded his arms. "All I'm saying is that, from what I've seen, housekeeping jobs require long hours and a lot of hard work. You can't deny that by a sheer stroke of luck you have—or had—the best job in St. Paul. Your employer creates very little work for you and he's pretty much granted you the run of the house. He's gone most of the time working on cases and giving you the place all to yourself. On top of that, you have me to do all your heavy lifting. You'll *never* find those ideal conditions again."

Much to my chagrin, I had to admit he was right. Working for an unmarried man who was gone a lot and who liked his nightlife was an easy job. Despite my issues with Miss Amundsen, I was fortunate to have found it. If only Gus hadn't ruined it all by showing up unexpectedly—

"Listen, Esther," he raised his palms in a gesture of peacemaking, "just because you were fired, that doesn't mean you don't deserve to get paid today. You need to come back to the house with me and ask for your wages. I know you didn't receive them."

I responded with a wry laugh. "I doubt Miss Amundsen would go for that."

"She's not the one who pays you. Besides, she's gone home, remember?"

His words were difficult to deny. What was I to do? My condition, as he had pointed out, had to take priority in my life. And every cent I earned would be needed...

"I really do need the money," I said thinking aloud.

"Then it's settled." He grabbed his hat. "Let's go."

The waitress suddenly arrived with my food. Before she had a chance to set it on the table, however, Daniel held up his hand. "Would you be so kind as to wrap it so we can take it with us? We have to leave."

"Absolutely!" She set the sandwich plate back on her tray. "Be back in a minute." She returned quickly with a paper sack and set it on the table.

I peered into the bag as I stood at the cash register, waiting for Daniel. He'd insisted on paying my bill. The sandwich had been wrapped in waxed paper and the soup had been put into a cardboard container. I decided to save it for an early dinner, instead.

On the way back to the house, Daniel carried my satchel. As we walked down the alley and neared the backyard, I saw Mr. Van Elsberg's shiny blue Chrysler sitting in the driveway and my stomach began to churn, strengthening my resolve to collect my pay and be on my way as quickly as possible. Going back inside that place would bring back the trauma of seeing Gus today and how I had stood so close to him I could have touched him. And he could have grabbed me.

Walking in the July heat, the thought gave me the chills.

*   *   *

Daniel and I entered through the back door of the house, our silence an indication of our somber moods. The place was so quiet it seemed deserted although the kitchen looked just as I had left it. A small pile of potatoes lay in the sink, turning gray from exposure to the air. On the counter next to it, a newspaper was spread open and covered with a mound of potato peels, the paring knife lying next to it.

Daniel removed his hat and set my satchel on the bottom step of the servants' stairway while I temporarily stored my lunch bag in the Frigidaire. We looked at each other, wondering what to do next then began to make our way through the house to find our employer. I hung back and allowed him to go first. We passed the small, first-floor lavatory, walked through the dining room and into the living room. From there, we went into the front parlor and that was when I signaled to Daniel that Mr. Van Elsberg was out on the front porch, standing at the railing and smoking a cigarette He seemed upset as he gazed at the cars parked along the street. I had only witnessed him smoking one other time since I'd started working for him, so it seemed a bit odd to me to see him doing it now. Some people smoked when they were nervous and I wondered if he was having second thoughts about working with such an explosive and unpredictable man as Gus.

The oppressive summer heat had turned the house into a huge oven this afternoon, even with the fans going so I understood why he'd want to smoke out there. Or was he waiting for me, expecting me to approach the house from the front sidewalk like I did the first time we met?

Daniel went to the screen door and opened it halfway. "She's here," was all he said.

Mr. Van Elsberg tossed what was left of his cigarette behind the rose bushes and walked into the house. He wore dark gray trousers and a matching vest over a starched, blue and white striped shirt with the sleeves rolled up and unbuttoned at the neck. His tall frame filled the doorway as he entered the foyer. He smiled briefly when our eyes met.

I clasped my hands together. "I've come for my pay."

Mr. Van Elsberg turned to Daniel. "Let's all go into the living room and talk, shall we? It's cooler in there with the fan going."

I gave Daniel a long look, wondering what was going on. He didn't meet my gaze. I followed the men into the living room, wondering why Mr. Van Elsberg was making such a production about paying me. Perhaps he planned to hold some back…

"Please, sit down."

I took a seat in one of the wing chairs facing the davenport, directly in the path of an oscillating fan. The low setting provided relief from the sultry air without disrupting our conversation. Daniel sat in the other chair.

"It's still rather hot in here," Mr. Van Elsberg said, rolling his sleeves a little higher. "I need a glass of ice water. No, don't get up, Esther. I'll get it. Would you like one?"

"Yes, please." I sat back down, surprised at his solicitousness.

"Daniel? Some water?"

Daniel nodded.

Mr. Van Elsberg returned in a few minutes with three tall glasses filled with ice cubes and chilled water from a pitcher I always kept in the Frigidaire. He handed me one, gave one to Daniel, and took a seat in the center of the davenport, facing me. A low, marble-topped table separated us.

"I apologize for what happened today," he said solemnly and set his glass on the table. "I realize I'm not around here much but I never authorized Louisa to supervise you when I'm gone. She was wrong to berate you for refusing to serve coffee to my client and then ordering you to leave because of it. She wasn't speaking for me."

"I didn't mean to be difficult. I was afraid to come back into the parlor," I said quietly. "Gus—I mean, your client—he frightened me."

This line of conversation made me uncomfortable. I didn't want to talk about Gus. I simply wanted my money so I could be on my way. Mr. Van Elsberg, however, didn't seem to be in any hurry. Daniel sat in his chair like a bump on a log and his silence irritated me. Was he there to help me get my money or not?

"I saw how you reacted when you delivered his coffee," Mr. Van Elsberg replied. "Mr. LeDoux is a rather outspoken man but his outburst was uncalled for in the presence of ladies. After Miss Amundsen left the room, I told him I'd be in contact with him and asked him not to return."

I stared in shock. He told my husband to leave? It took a man with a lot of confidence to pull that off…

"The incident will not be repeated," he said soberly and leaned forward, resting his elbows on his knees. "You have my word."

"You're not taking on his case?" Though it was clearly none of my business and I risked being put in my place, I had to ask.

"Yes, I am," he said, "but because of who I'm dealing with, I've decided to handle this one differently. He and I will conduct our business at another location. I don't want you or Miss Amundsen to feel afraid in my home ever again."

"Are you saying—"

"I'm saying I want you to stay and continue to work for me. I have no quarrel with your performance, Esther. You're a good, dependable housekeeper and an even better cook." He flashed a disarming smile. "And you're terrific when it comes to entertaining. I'd be crazy to let you go."

I hadn't expected *this*. I just wanted to get paid.

"But…what about Miss Amundsen? She'll be angry when she hears you've asked me to stay. She was difficult to work with even before today. Now the situation will be worse."

His quick frown revealed his frustration over being dragged into the middle of female squabbles. "Don't concern yourself with her. Starting on Monday, she'll only be working in the morning. Surely you two can get along for that short amount of time."

I took a sip of my chilled water. "I have no problem working with her, but she's always looking for something to use against me."

He dismissed my objection with a wave of his hand. "If a problem arises, you come to me and I'll take care of it, all right?"

I bit my lip, amazed at how much this new arrangement was about to change the situation around here. Even so, there was still the problem of Daniel knowing about my condition. Would he eventually tell my boss? I only told him because I never thought I'd see him again. "Well, I…"

My hesitation prompted Mr. Van Elsberg to jam his hand into his pocket and pull out a wad of bills. "I'll raise your pay by two dollars a week." He counted out my week's pay and added the additional dollars. He set the money on the table and pushed it toward me. "I'm serious, Esther. I don't want to lose you."

"…and I'm not subject to Miss Amundsen's threats or intimidation any longer?"

"No," he replied with finality. "You handle the kitchen. I'll handle her."

"Okay." I let out a sigh of relief, glad to be back into my old routine minus the harassment from his small-minded secretary. The additional pay would come in handy, too. Again, my only regret was telling Daniel about the baby. I'd portrayed myself as a cheap doxy in his eyes, but there was no way I could set him straight by telling him the truth.

"Good. Now that we have that business out of the way and things are back to normal," Mr. Van Elsberg said as he stood, "I'm having a few people over tomorrow night for dinner before we go to the theater. Around six o'clock."

I stood as well, my mind already exploring a few new menu ideas. "How many?"

"I'm expecting eight people, including me."

I checked the pendulum clock on the wall for the time. "Then I'd better get moving. I have to make a trip to the market before they close."

Daniel stood last, clapping his hat back on his head. "I'd better get the yard mowed and fix the gate on the porch." He patted my shoulder. "Glad to have you back."

I laughed, knowing he was happily anticipating the opportunity to sample all of the delicacies tomorrow as I prepared them for the party.

Daniel left the room. With nothing left to say, I retrieved the empty glasses off the table, making notes in my head about items to put on my grocery list.

"By the way," Mr. Van Elsberg said as he gazed down at me, his eyes softening, "you look very nice today."

I was still wearing my green outfit. "Thank you, Mr. Van—"

"From now on, when it's just the two of us, you can call me Will."

I smiled, warmed by his offer. "All right…Will. I'll remember that."

I understood we needed to keep our relationship formal around other people, especially Miss Amundsen, to avoid gossip. Having a young woman working and living under a single man's roof was probably raising eyebrows among Will's neighbors and friends anyway, but he had always been a gentleman around me so propriety didn't matter as far as I was concerned. I had no qualms about being alone with him.

80

"I'll go upstairs and change back into my uniform before I go out," I said, eager to get started on the party preparations.

"Hold on." Will handed me a couple more bills. "While you're out and about today, buy yourself some new uniforms. Louisa promised me weeks ago she'd purchase some for you, but she hasn't done it so I'm counting on you to get your own instead. Get whatever you want, but make sure they fit right. Throw away those ugly things you've been wearing. They remind me of *Whistler's Mother*. I never want to see them again. Understand?"

I laughed. "With pleasure!"

I stared into Will's intense blue eyes and thought about what a good catch he'd make for the right woman someday. He was smart, handsome, and charming, but above all, a decent man.

Like Gus had been…before prohibition.

Chapter Seven

I ate my sandwich with more chilled water while drawing up my list of dishes for the party and a subsequent list of all the groceries to get for the meal. Then I walked swiftly to the market on Selby Avenue and ordered them, but was told because of the late hour, the food could not be delivered until first thing tomorrow morning.

Fine. Since I couldn't cook, I hopped on the streetcar and went to a shop on University Avenue to buy my new uniforms. On the way there, I closed my eyes and relaxed, but couldn't help thinking about what Mr. Van—er…Will had said to me earlier. Did I really look like *Whistler's Mother* in that ragamuffin dress Miss Amundsen had forced me to wear? I almost laughed out loud. Suppressing the urge, I smiled to myself instead. Not anymore!

I didn't have to address Will's secretary as Miss Amundsen any longer, either, now that I knew our positions were equal. They probably always had been equal, but she had made it clear to me from the first day of my employment that she considered herself in charge. It was obvious she had never intended to purchase any new uniforms for me. Rather, she'd sought to humiliate and embarrass me by making me wear ugly, oversized gowns so I'd become disillusioned with the situation and leave.

What a sad, depressing woman, I thought to myself as the breeze from the open window cooled my face. Will's sister, Madeline had proclaimed Louisa was in love with Will. It had been obvious to me right off the bat. However, for a woman as intelligent and capable as Louisa was, she didn't know anything about how to attract a man. A sugary sweet voice couldn't make up for a sour, insecure personality.

I wondered what her reaction would be when she found out I'd gone over her head again and shopped for the uniforms myself.

Green with envy. Plotting her next scheme to do away with me...

I sighed and cleared all negative thoughts of that small-minded woman from my mind. Today had started badly but turned around in a good way. I wanted to stay in that frame of mind.

*   *   *

The next morning, I rose at dawn, waiting for the grocery delivery so I could start preparing my dishes for the party. I hadn't seen Will since yesterday afternoon. He'd gone out, presumably working on his new case, and hadn't returned until late last night. I'd heard him leave again early in the morning before I came downstairs. When I arrived in the kitchen to fix breakfast for Daniel, I found Will had already made a pot of coffee and it was still hot. It bothered me to know he was looking into my disappearance, but I truly didn't believe the trail of evidence would lead back to me. How could it? I'd been extremely careful in keeping both my identity and my whereabouts secret. Even my mother didn't know where I lived now or where I had been for the month preceding my employment here. Once Will had exhausted all avenues and told Gus I had vanished off the face of the earth, would Gus stop searching for me?

Will arrived home later that afternoon but went right upstairs to change and promptly leave again. Though I didn't see him come in, his heavy footsteps on the stairway alerted me he'd arrived. I was busy frosting a cake at the time and had much more to do, so I paid little attention to him.

Just before six o'clock, I ran upstairs to change into my evening uniform. It was more formal with long sleeves, a white, pointed lace collar, and a matching lace apron with a square front. I'd purchased two black uniforms, complete with aprons and light stockings, spending all the money Will had given me. Both dresses had an elastic waist; both were a perfect fit.

Will and his guests arrived while I was changing. I had everything ready, but because of the heat, had not planned to set out the food until they appeared. Earlier, the iceman had delivered several chunks of ice and I had set them in pans, placing one in front of each of the electric fans to help cool the air. In the living room, I had placed an ice bucket, glasses, and several bottles of ginger ale for the guests to mix with their whiskey.

I descended the servants' stairway at promptly six o'clock to find everyone in the back yard, posing for pictures with Madeline's new "folding" Brownie camera.

"Esther, come out here!" she said when she saw me peering through the screen door. I was curious about what they were doing. "We need you to take our picture!"

Will and Peter were examining the camera when I opened the door and came down the back steps. Madeline turned to speak to me and exclaimed, "Well, look at *you*. Turn around now and let me see your new outfit." Had I looked so atrocious in my old dress that even Will's sister noticed? Madeline put her hands on my shoulders and literally pivoted me in a circle to get a better look, embarrassing me. "It's about time that cheap brother of mine spent some money on you and gave you decent uniforms. You look much better."

Will merely chuckled and shook his head at her remark.

"Seriously, Esther," she said as she took the camera from Will's hands and handed it to me. "Do you know how to use one of these?"

"Yes," I said and told her I'd owned one myself in the past.

84

Madeline took charge of the group and had the women sit on lawn chairs with their men standing behind them. I looked through the lens, ready to take the shot when I hesitated, realizing Gloria wasn't present. Will stood behind a different blonde. I wondered if they'd had a falling out…

I took the group picture and handed the camera back to Madeline. She then began instructing one of the women to pose on the back steps for a solo portrait. I hurried past her; my head filled with a dozen details to follow up on before they came into the house for dinner. In my haste to leave, I failed to notice she was ready to shoot the picture. Suddenly I heard the clicking sound of her finger pressing the shutter button.

"Oops!" Madeline looked up. "I need to do it again. Esther, I accidentally got you in the picture."

I spun around, mortified to have ruined her photograph. "I'm so sorry! I should have been more careful!"

She waved me off. "My hand jerked when I pressed the button so the picture wouldn't have come out centered anyway. I'll just toss this one out when I get the film developed."

I hurried to the front of the house and came in through the porch, eager to get the meal on the table and fade into the background. Given the present heat we were enduring, I made all cold food for a picnic-style dinner. By the time the group trooped into the house I had the dining room table ready and stood back, waiting in case Will's guests needed anything else. As I had suspected, they chose not to sit at the table, but instead filled their plates and went into the living room to eat, where it was cooler.

Around seven o'clock, I held the front door for Will and his friends as they left the house and headed for the theater. He was the last one to leave. He snatched his light-colored Panama hat from the coat tree, placed it at an angle on his head, and whispered in my ear as he walked past me, "Well done—as always." I mustered the energy to smile but when I shut the door behind him, I slumped against it, totally exhausted.

It took an hour to clean up the party dishes and straighten the house. I turned off all of the lights except the small lamp in the foyer and slowly climbed the two flights of stairs to my room. I changed clothes, brushed my teeth, and fell upon my bed wearing a light dressing gown and holding a wet, folded towel in my hand. The small oscillating fan and ice—taken from the dining room—provided a little relief from the stifling temperature in my bedroom. As I lay on my bed, I was reminded that my baby was growing and my condition would one day be impossible to hide.

"Dear God, what am I going to do," I whispered to the shadowed ceiling. "Where can I go to have this baby and be safe?" Deep in my spirit, I heard a still, small voice as though God was actually answering me.

Go to Mamma's house…

I placed the wet towel on my forehead to help cool me down. Why would God tell me to go there? It wasn't safe! If I moved in with Mamma, I could take care of her—yes—but it wouldn't take long for Gus to catch on, even if I never left the house. The visiting nurse would probably inform him right away that I'd come home and he'd be breaking down the door to accost me like the gangster he'd become.

The thought of even being in the same room with him again made the hair stand up on my arms. I closed my eyes and slipped into a deep, troubled sleep.

* * *

On Monday morning, Louisa failed to show up for work. I'd never known her to take a day off and her absence concerned me.

I approached Will about it at nine o'clock, just as he was preparing to leave. "Where is Louisa today? I hope she's not ill."

"She's taking some time off," he replied as he strapped on his shoulder holster. "She'll be back next week."

Whoopee. It'll be nice and relaxed for a change…

I wondered if she planned to spend the week looking for a new job.

Will slipped into his suit coat and grabbed his hat. "See you later." He grinned, tipping it toward me in a friendly salute. "Don't wait up for me."

I laughed and shut the screen door behind him. Ever since the day Will convinced me to stay on, our private relationship had relaxed to the point where he often teased me. I didn't see much of him, but when I did, he treated me more as a friend now than an employee.

My relationship with Daniel had evolved into a closer friendship as well. He made good on his promise to help me with all of the heavy lifting around the house and on Mondays carried baskets of washed sheets and towels out to the backyard for me to hang on the clothesline. He also took out the trash, moved furniture, and reached for things on the upper shelves in the pantry so I didn't have to climb on a chair to get them. Never once did he mention my condition or allow me to thank him. In return, I made his favorite meals and baked treats for his morning coffee break.

I had grown to trust these men and enjoy their company. I wished this arrangement could go on forever, but I knew in my heart that I couldn't continue my friendship with either of these men once I left this house. It made me sad.

On Wednesday, I finished my daily chores by noon and went upstairs to change into my green outfit for the rest of the day. I planned to stop at Big Louie's for ice cream then hop on the streetcar to visit Mamma and Francie.

To my surprise, Will's car pulled into the driveway just as I emerged from the back door. He smiled as I walked toward the vehicle. "Where are you going all dressed up?"

"My first stop is Big Louie's. I'm dying for ice cream. Then I'm off to visit somebody."

"Ice cream, huh?" He winked as he slid out of the car and closed the door. "Better watch out. All that sugar will give you a toothache." We laughed. "I'll be heading out again in about ten minutes. Would you like a lift?"

His question about my afternoon plans had been asked in a friendly way, but I was wary of talking about myself. I kept on walking past the car. "It's a nice day. I think I'll walk."

He frowned at my answer, as though he was disappointed. "See you later, then."

I turned back and teased him with the line he usually said to me. "Don't wait up for me!"

He laughed and gave me a "thumbs up" as he walked along the sidewalk to the back entrance.

At Big Louie's, I ordered a "Chocolate Temptation" sundae and savored every spoonful of the rich dark syrup topping mixed with marshmallow crème. Scraping the bottom of the tulip glass, I marveled over how much I'd grown to obsess over ice cream. I stopped at Big Louie's every chance I could. Of course, it didn't help that my favorite soda shop was located only two blocks away.

By the time I arrived at Mamma's place, it was nearly two o'clock. I slipped through the alley, nervously watching for Gus' car or any vehicle that looked suspicious to me. By the time I reached the back door of the house, I was sweating and out of breath. I ran up the back steps and jerked open the screen door, bursting into the kitchen.

Francie stood at the sink doing laundry with a small washboard. She spun around when the screen door banged shut, her face brightening. "Hi, Char!"

I collapsed into a kitchen chair and rested my elbows on the table, gasping for breath.

"What's the matter?"

"Nothing. I hope." I drew in a deep breath and pulled off my hat. My glasses were next. I folded them and tucked them inside the hat. "I just ran all the way down the alley. I wanted to get here as quickly as I could in case Gus is lurking around."

Francie wiped her soapy hands on a towel. "He does spy on us sometimes. He thinks we don't see him parked down the street, but I notice everything."

I began to worry. "I wonder if he's there now."

Francie threw down her towel. "I'll go and see." She went into the living room and stepped out the front door, peering around the tall arborvitae bush next to the front steps.

"Nope," she said as she walked back into the kitchen. "He's not there today."

I relaxed a little. "How's Mamma? I didn't hear her radio going so I looked in on her while you were out of the room and saw she was asleep."

"About the same." Francie sat down at the table; her youthful face looking crestfallen. "The nurse says that in her condition, it's to be expected, but Mamma is so tired all the time." Her wide blue eyes filled with worry. "I don't know what I'll do if she…"

I scooted to the chair next to hers and wrapped my arms around her. "Don't think about that now." I hugged her tight. "You never know. She could be stronger than we realize. She's bound and determined to hold the baby in her arms one day."

Francie sniffed and rubbed her nose. "I suppose." I could tell she didn't believe it. Sadly, neither did I. "Oh," Francie said, her eyes widening as she straightened. "I almost forgot. A man came around asking questions about you!"

I froze. "When?"

"Last Friday, in the afternoon."

"What's his name?"

Francie nodded. "I don't remember it now, but he gave us a card. I'll get it for you."

She jumped up and began rummaging through one of the cabinet drawers. "Here it is." She spun around and handed it to me. The business card belonged to Will.

"So, he's a private detective," I said, pretending I didn't know him. I looked up. "What kinds of questions did he ask?"

"He wanted to know if we've seen you since your nightclub closed and if we knew where you were now." She shrugged. "We said we didn't know where you were—and that was the truth."

I set the card on the table. "Did he ask if you knew whether I was alive or dead?"

"Yeah." Francie slid into her chair again. "Mamma acted like she was going to faint and he apologized for bringing up a sensitive subject."

I smiled. Mamma knew how to handle the tough detective.

Someday I'd have to sit Francie down and have a talk with her about Mamma's eventual departure from this world and how it would change her own circumstances, but I decided to wait. The less Francie thought about it until the time actually came, the better. I didn't want to burden her young soul with such a heavy subject.

I helped with the wash and made supper to give Francie a break. Mamma woke while we were cooking and said she was hungry. We set up the small parlor table in her bedroom so the three of us could dine together and listen to a radio show.

I took my leave at dusk but promised I'd come back again next week.

With my glasses on and my hat pulled past my ears, I went down the back steps and made my way through the narrow backyard. Just as I neared the corner of the garage, I heard a car turn into the alley. Something about it put my senses on alert. Without looking back, I turned and ran as fast as I could past the garage, sprinting past the house. The car's brakes squealed as it came to a screeching halt next to the garage. I knew without a doubt it was Gus.

I ran through the front yard and across to the front of the neighbor's house, hoping Gus didn't have another car watching the street. Determined to get away at all costs, I weaved through the neighboring yards, using garages and parked cars as a shield as Gus' vehicle zoomed up and down the block searching for me. I didn't stop until I'd run for three blocks, but by that time, my head swam with dizziness and I had to slow down. A stitch ached in my side from running and my heart hammered so hard in my chest it thundered in my ears.

This is insane…

Not knowing what else to do, I kept walking until darkness descended. Then I caught the streetcar and went home. The streetcar dropped me off under the glowing lights on the busy corner of Selby Avenue and Dale Street. Not taking any chances, I ran across the street as soon as I caught a break in the traffic and kept going until I reached the backyard of Will's house.

His car was gone. The back of the house was dark, but Daniel's lights shone through the basement windows. I saw a figure lurking on the back steps and stopped short. A man moved swiftly toward me. I began to back up, ready to scream.

"Evening, Esther," Daniel said quietly, approaching me. "Go into the house and straight up to your room. *Stay there.*"

"What's going on?" I whispered as he clutched my forearm and guided me to the house.

"Never you mind. Just do as I say. Mr. Van Elsberg is on his way home."

He practically pulled me up the stairs and shoved me through the back door. "Lock the door and *go upstairs. Now.*"

Given the way he was acting, I wondered if Will was in trouble somehow. Frightened and unsettled, I did what I was told and quickly went into the kitchen. The only light on in the house came from a small lamp in the foyer. That one always stayed on until Will came home.

I went directly up the servant's stairway to my floor and stopped in the lavatory. As a precaution, I pulled down the shade on the small window in the back wall but didn't turn on the light. After I finished brushing my teeth in the dark, I made my way to my room, still wearing the green outfit I liked so much. Now that I'd been seen wearing it, the garment would get laundered and go into a box, never to be worn by me again.

Both windows in my room were open and a warm breeze stirred the curtains. I sat on the bed and rubbed my tired face with my hands.

What a terrible day...

After what happened at Mamma's place, I didn't feel safe leaving the house anymore. I'd escaped tonight but what about next time? If Gus thought he'd seen me, he'd be extra vigilant about watching for me now. I couldn't take that chance again.

Discouraged, I lay down on the bed with a tired sigh and tried to take my mind off my troubles by wondering why Will was on his way home and why Daniel found it necessary to act so secretively about it. Nothing seemed amiss as far as I could tell and again, I wondered if Will was in some kind of trouble.

A strong flutter quickened deep in my belly. I'd been experiencing this new phenomenon for a week now. At first, I didn't know what it was, but the second time it happened, I realized my baby had begun to make his presence known. Grateful for the little guy's timely diversion, I rested my hand on the tiny bump under my navel and breathed in slowly, relaxing for the first time in hours.

"Sleep well, Julien," I whispered to my baby as I closed my eyes and exhaled a deep breath. Convinced I had a boy growing inside me, I'd already named the child and had started talking to him whenever he moved. How nice it would be, I thought, when I could hold this little one in my arms and talk to him or sing him to sleep—

The sharp "click" of a car door shutting jerked me back to my present reality by alerting me to some new activity going on in the front of the house. I raised my weary body to a sitting position, wondering if Will had parked at the curb, intending to drop in temporarily and leave again. That idea posed a problem, however, because I had not heard a car arrive. The neighborhood seemed unusually quiet tonight.

Curious, I stood up and peered through the screen to the street below. The scene unfolding in front of the house instantly shattered my momentary bliss. Gus' Phaeton sat parked at the curb. My husband stood on the sidewalk, looking upward.

Chapter Eight

"Dear God, *no...*" I whispered to myself as I stepped back from the window, my heart catching in my throat. "What is *he* doing here?" Will had made a point of informing me he'd told Gus never to come to his home again. Why, then, was Gus standing on the sidewalk, waiting for Will to let him in?

He must have recognized me when he saw me running away...

Or did he plan to fire Will because he'd hired someone else whom he believed would give him faster, conclusive results?

Daniel had given me strict orders to stay in my room, but I wouldn't hear a word of the conversation up here, and I *had* to know what Gus and Will were talking about. I jerked off my nightgown and slipped on my maid uniform. Since it was nearly all black, it would blend into the shadows better.

My feet made a soft pitter-patter on the wood floor as I hurried barefoot down the hallway to the back of the house and took the servants' stairs to the second floor. From there I went to the bedroom at the front of the house, situated just below mine, and looked out the bay window at the street. I couldn't see Gus anywhere, now, and wondered if he'd gone to the front porch to wait in the shadows.

I hurried across the hallway and descended the main stairway. The

94

steps creaked under my feet, prompting me to slow down. Once I reached the bottom, I moved stealthily across the oak landing to the small alcove tucked next to the front entry doors.

I slipped into the tiny, oval-shaped room too fast and bumped into a small half-round console table. The miniature Tiffany lamp on it moved sideways, but I caught it before it slid off and hit the floor. I held still for a few moments, hoping no one had heard me stumbling around like a bull in a china shop. Then I stood up and backed into a parlor chair that was positioned against the opposite wall. So much for being discrete!

Sheer curtains hung in the oriel window that faced the porch. I'd peeked through this window the day I came to the house to apply for a job. Moving slowly, I knelt on the floor and rested my hands on the window sill as I leaned forward, raising just enough to peer through the hem of the sheer curtain. Gus and two gun-toting henchmen were on the porch. Gus' large silhouette stood out as he paced back and forth. Darkness prevented me from seeing his expression, but the taut line of his shoulders and the rigidness in his stride revealed his pent-up anxiety.

My trepidation rose with each of his footsteps. I told myself to be strong, but the powerful and ruthless aura emanating from Gus—and the small, but deadly army that surrounded him—shattered my sense of security once again. Familiar enemies, fear, and despondency were like shackles around my soul. Would I ever *really* be free of this man? What would it take to force him to accept my disappearance and let me go?

The back door suddenly burst open and two sets of footsteps thundered through the house. The small lamp in the foyer cast a dim shadow across the outside wall of the alcove and I began to panic, afraid Daniel and Will would see me hiding there as they marched into the foyer. I flattened against the inside wall between the table and the window seat, hoping my narrow frame would blend into the shadows.

"Turn on a light in the parlor then shut the windows and draw the shades," Will told Daniel as they rushed into the foyer. "I'll get the door."

The parlor suddenly filled with light, spilling across the foyer to the landing as Daniel went about quickly shutting the windows and pulling down the shades. Will jerked the front door open and went into the entryway to open the screen door.

"It's about time you got here," Gus said, his voice a low growl echoing through the house. "I don't like to be kept waiting." Their footfalls advanced into the parlor. His henchmen remained outside, standing guard at the door.

Taking great pains to be quiet, I stealthily crept to the corner of the alcove and placed my hands flat on the wall for support then peeked around the edge to watch the men gathering in the parlor.

"We agreed you wouldn't come to my home again," Will said tersely, his hands balled at his sides. "Do you realize what time it is? I don't want my neighbors complaining about strangers lurking on my front porch after dark. If one of them called the police—"

"I could care less what time it is," Gus roared. "This is important! If the cops show up, I'll take care of it. They won't arrest me or report me to the Feds. They're still on my payroll." He gestured toward Daniel standing at the edge of the room watching Gus like a hawk. "Who is he and what's he doing here?"

"Daniel Blythe works for me." Will glanced at Daniel and nodded toward the kitchen. "Leave us, Dan."

Daniel scrutinized Gus with distrust. "You sure, boss?"

"Yeah, it's okay," Will said. "I'll call you if I need anything else."

Daniel shot a parting frown at Gus then reluctantly left the parlor by way of the living room and went on through the dining room to the kitchen. I heard the basement door open and close.

"All right. What is so important it can't wait 'til tomorrow?" Will swept back the panels of his coat, placing his hands on his hips. "This had better be good, LeDoux."

Gus' eyes widened. "I saw her."

Will froze, taken aback. "You did? Where?"

"At her mother's house—in the alley. She turned and ran when she saw me. Gave me the slip when she disappeared between the houses."

Will pushed the brim of his hat back with the tip of his thumb. "Are you sure it was her?"

Gus reached into the pocket of his coat and pulled out his flask. "You heard what I said."

"Did you see her face?"

Gus shrugged. "Well, no, but..."

"Then you can't be *certain.*"

"Look, Van Elsberg," Gus said as he unscrewed the cap of his flask, "I've been married to the woman for nine years. I *know* her shape from the back and how she moves. It was her all right." He put the flask to his lips and took a long swallow without batting an eye.

Will leaned against the edge of his desk, folding his arms. "All right, then, just for argument's sake, we'll assume it was her. What was she wearing?"

Gus shrugged again. "A green dress."

"Most women own some type of green dress, Gus. Is that all you saw? I need something more specific than that. Any distinguishable markings on the dress? Any accessories? Something that stood out to you?"

"She may have been wearing a hat." Gus took another swig of whiskey.

"Was she pregnant?"

Gus set his flask on the parlor table and pulled out his cigarettes. "I couldn't tell from the back."

Will cocked one brow. "Were you sober at the time?"

Gus let out a string of profanity in French as his answer to the question.

Will shook his head. "You're not giving me much to go on."

"I told you everything I know," Gus replied irascibly. "I don't remember anything else. I was shocked to see her and when she disappeared so fast, I didn't have time to think about making a note of specific details. That's *your* job!"

Will let out a tense sigh, obviously tired of Gus' theatrics. "Go home and get some sleep, LeDoux. You look worn out and it's possible you've mistaken someone else for her."

"If the woman wasn't my wife then why did she run away?"

"Can you blame her?" Will let out a wry chuckle. "You probably scared the living daylights out of some poor girl, chasing after her like that." His expression took on a serious note. "Regarding your wife, I've questioned her friends and family. So far, no one knows where she went or what happened to her so I'm spreading the net wider." He stood up. "I'll start by going back to all of the neighbors on her mother's block again to see if anybody saw her tonight."

"I want some answers *soon*," Gus said, an unlit Lucky Strike dangling from his lips. He pointed toward the large bay window. "I know now she's out there somewhere. So, find her and bring her back to me."

"You know as well as I do, Gus," Will argued as he removed his hat and dropped it on his desk, "if she is alive and purposely eluding you, there's a good chance she won't agree to come back to you."

"Yeah, well, I'm not paying *you* to give her that option." Gus fished a small matchbox from his jacket pocket. "Your job is to find out where she's holed up and bring her back!"

Will stood face to face with Gus, gripping his hands on his hips. "I don't kidnap people, LeDoux. That wasn't part of our agreement."

Gus opened the box and pulled out a wooden match. "Well, if you don't have the stomach for it," he replied in a mocking tone, "let me know where she is and I'll fetch her myself. Makes no difference to me."

"What do you plan on doing with her once I locate her—that is if she *is* still alive?"

Gus struck the match and cupped his hands in front of his face to light his cigarette. Once the tip of his cigarette glowed red, he shook the match to distinguish it. He took a drag and blew the smoke away. His eyes narrowed. "You leave that to me."

A chill coursed down my spine. I turned around, pushing my back flat against the wall. I'd heard all I could handle of this conversation and wanted to go back to my room, but I couldn't leave, not without them seeing me. Instead, I tiptoed carefully back around the table and stood wedged between the table and the window seat with my back to the wall, waiting desperately for the meeting to end.

"I'll contact you as soon as I get some new information," Will said in a tone that suggested their discussion had run its course. "In the meantime, if you need to speak with me, call first and we'll set up a conference at Harv Katzenbaum's office. In any case, don't show up here again."

Gus' heavy footfalls pounded to the front door and stopped. "You've got seven days Van Elsberg. No more. If you're as good as everyone says you are, you'll find her by then. If not, maybe you won't be in business any longer."

"Don't threaten me," I heard Will say in a low, steel-soft voice.

"Don't fail *me*," Gus countered, his tone as brutal as his words.

The front door creaked open. Gus' footsteps echoed through the entryway, out the screen door, and onto the porch. He paused, standing so close to the long, narrow window next to me I could hear him drag on his cigarette.

Pressed ramrod straight against the wall, I covered my face with my hands, afraid to breathe lest he heard me. It seemed like forever until his footsteps scuffed across the porch and quickly bounded down the steps.

Inside the house, Will's long strides stomped through the parlor as he unleashed a murderous string of profanity. I blinked, stunned by his reaction to Gus' threat. Never before had I witnessed this much anger coming from him. A drawer slid open in his desk. I heard the clinking sound of a bottle being hastily removed. Then the drawer slammed shut. The parlor light snapped off and his footsteps crossed the room. A loud thud startled me, sounding like a small explosion, but I knew Will had just jammed his fist against the sliding door as he passed through the entrance into the foyer. Without bothering to extinguish the foyer light, Will bounded onto the landing. I held my breath, melting against the wall, but he didn't see me nor did he even look my way. With the bottle of whiskey in his right hand, he took the stairs two at a time to the second floor.

The moment his footfalls began to fade, I ran from the alcove with the speed of a gunshot and sprinted through the house to the back stairway. I tiptoed up the stairs as fast as I could and on the second floor, moved quickly in case Will left his bedroom to use the lavatory and caught me sneaking around. Sliding up the wall, I stepped on the inside edge of the oak treads to minimize the creak of the wood. Once I reached my floor, I tiptoed down the hallway to my room and peered out the window. Gus' car had driven away, but his threat remained fresh in my memory.

"What do you plan on doing with her once I locate her—that is if she is still alive?"

100

Gus' eyes narrowed. "You leave that to me."

Knowing what it could mean to be on the receiving end of my husband's deep-seated anger, I collapsed upon my bed, buried my face in the pillow, and cried myself to sleep.

* * *

For the next several days, Will left early in the morning—before breakfast—and didn't return until late in the evening. On Saturday morning, I managed to catch him before he left the house and asked him if he would be bringing guests home that night. For my trouble, I received a quick, terse response on the order of, "No. I'll let you know when I decide to have another party." Obviously, his investigation wasn't bearing the fruit he'd hoped it would. After that, I went quietly about my work and spoke as little to him as possible. I couldn't tell what upset him more; his failure to locate me or the blow coming to his reputation if he ultimately came up empty-handed. These were trying days for Will Van Elsberg.

The morning paper arrived late, adding even more fuel to Will's uncharacteristically grumpy mood. He'd been gone for an hour before I heard the folded bundle hit the porch. Normally, I didn't pay much attention to it. I had too much work to do to stand around reading the day's news. Today, however, as I retrieved it off the mat in front of the screen door, I stared at the headline and couldn't believe my eyes.

What happened to Charlotte LeDoux?

The wife of Gus "Lucky" LeDoux is still missing.

The center of the page held a large picture of me wearing the silvery blue, beaded hat I had worn on the night Federal agents raided La Coquette. My glamorous look included plenty of cosmetics such as eyeliner, mascara, and cherry red lipstick. I didn't remember this shot being taken. The reporter obviously had snapped it outdoors when I was unaware of being photographed.

I quickly read through the article looking for any information that might hint at my whereabouts, but the writer expressed acute dismay at the lack of evidence leading to a determination of whether I was alive or dead.

Whoooooh...

Gus couldn't definitively claim he'd seen me and Will couldn't find any trail leading to me. In a couple of days, Will's final week to locate me would expire. If he came up empty-handed, my husband would be angry and disappointed, but Will's agreement with Gus would be fulfilled. That said, I wasn't naïve. I didn't doubt for a minute Gus would accept Will's findings. He'd probably hire someone else to take over the case, but at least he would *never* come back to this house again.

That little tidbit of good news certainly didn't solve all of my problems. It only took care of one. I still had to figure out how to visit Mamma without getting caught. Dress like her nurse, perhaps? Pondering over it made me nervous—and hungry for something sweet. I went into the kitchen and baked a blueberry pie.

*   *   *

On Monday morning, Louisa reported for work at eight o'clock sharp, looking dour as usual even though she wore a new midnight blue dress with a white lace collar; a completely new fashion for her. The moment her gaze rested upon me she drew back. "What's been going on while I've been gone?" No mention of her firing me or Will rehiring me.

"What do you mean?"

She gave me the once over with a disapproving sneer, as though my presence had somehow offended her. I looked down and realized she was appraising my new uniform. My daytime attire had elbow-length sleeves with a white, rounded collar and matching cuffs. The apron had a V front and scalloped edges. Best of all, the hem fell just below my knees. "Oh, this," I replied carelessly. "Mr. Van Elsberg decided I was due for a wardrobe change. When he hired me back, he gave me the money to buy what I wanted and told me he never wanted to see those old rags on me ever again." I kept the *Whistler's Mother* joke to myself.

"Hmmm... I *see.*"

"Did you have an enjoyable time off?"

She bristled. "Why do you care?"

I had all I could do to keep my mouth from calling her a few derogatory names in French. She hadn't been in the house five minutes yet her ugliness had already turned my good attitude into a dark, mutinous mood. "Actually, Louisa, I don't care at all. I rather enjoyed not having to put up with you for five days."

The lines around her mouth tightened. "Of all the arrogance. That's *Miss Amundsen* to you."

I gave her a cold smile. "All right, and you may call me *Miss Smith* from now on."

Her face darkened. "That will be the day..."

Will bounded down the front stairs into the foyer. "Oh, good morning, Louisa. I'm glad you're back." He walked into the parlor. "I've got a mountain of dictation on the notes from my present case for you to transcribe."

"Wonderful. I'll be right there," she replied in that phony, sickly-sweet voice she reserved only for him. She turned to me, a snide grin turning up the corners of her narrow lips as she whispered, "I knew my absence would make him realize just how much he needed me."

I shook my head and returned to the kitchen, determined to stay as far away from her as possible from now on. That woman had no idea what it took to convince a man to need her...

I had just pulled out the washing machine to launder bedding and towels when the telephone rang. Normally I didn't pay the slightest bit of attention to Will's phone calls, but this one sounded different. Instead of his usual business demeanor, he'd adopted a softer, more jovial tone. A few minutes later, he walked into the kitchen to get a fresh cup of coffee. "Maddie is joining me for lunch today," he said, using the nickname he called his sister. "She'll be here at noon." He picked up the coffee pot and poured himself a full cup. "She wants you to make those ham sandwiches you served us a couple of weeks ago."

Good, I thought. I didn't want to do the wash today anyway.

I smiled sweetly, knowing Louisa stood at the parlor door jealously watching us. "All right. Any other requests?"

"No," he replied, giving me a handsome grin. "Surprise us."

"I'd love to," I said and began to push the washer back into the far end of the pantry. "I'll get going to the market right away."

"Lunch with Madeline sounds wonderful!" Louisa said, standing inside the kitchen doorway. Her hint for an invitation had fallen on deaf ears, however. Will walked past her and went back into the parlor to continue working.

Ignoring her as well, I turned my back to her and scribbled a couple of ideas of what I planned to make then added the ingredients to my weekly shopping list. Stuffing the scrap of paper into my uniform pocket, I replaced my headband with my hat and took off for the market.

Forty-five minutes later I returned, breathless from hurrying, with the groceries I needed to make lunch. I'd arranged for the rest of the order to be delivered later that afternoon so as not to interfere with the timing of the meal. In the meantime, I had a lot of work to do and I immediately began to mix the ingredients for a special cake.

Madeline arrived a few minutes early and breezed through the front door smiling as though she hadn't a care in the world. She wore a butter-yellow pleated skirt and a yellow, drop waist blouse covered with large black polka dots. On her feet were black, pointed-toed shoes accented with square, silver buckles. "Hello, Will," she said with a

104

flourish as she walked into the parlor and kissed her brother on the cheek. "I know I'm a little early, but I thought we could have a drink before lunch." She pulled off her hat and fluffed her short, black hair as she walked out of the parlor, ignoring Louisa completely. "Esther, I smell something wonderful baking in your kitchen!"

I already had the dining room table set with china, crystal, and linens for two. I entered the living room with a tray containing two crystal lowball glasses and a small crystal ice bucket filled to the brim with ice cubes. Madeline had closed the heavy sliding doors between the living room and the parlor and I suspected her motivation was more to keep Louisa out of their conversation than to give the woman privacy to conduct her work.

"Louisa, you're excused for the day," Will said tactfully as he reopened the doors. "I'll see you tomorrow."

I placed a small vase of freshly cut flowers in the center of the dining room table and fussed with the settings as Will poured a drink for him and his sister. They commenced talking as though they were the only two people in the house.

With an angry, hurt look on her face, Louisa slammed her stenographer book on her desk and took her leave, letting the screen door bang on her way out.

"Honestly, Will," Madeline said as Louisa descended the front steps and disappeared. "I don't know what you see in her. That woman is positively *odious*."

Will sat on the sofa, stretching his arms across the back. "She has her good points."

Madeline leaned against the Victor credenza and sipped her drink. "I fail to see any."

"I wouldn't have kept her employed this long if she didn't."

Madeline swirled the ice in her glass. "You're always defending her! I don't understand why but she has such a hold over you."

Will laughed. "Did it ever occur to you, Maddie, that Louisa is very good at secretarial work? She does an excellent job and that's what matters most."

I went into the kitchen to dish up the plates for lunch as they continued to talk.

"Peter's secretary does an excellent job, too," Madeline argued, "and she can easily handle another person. Look, Will, Peter is serious about sharing an office with you. Why won't you consider it? You do so much work for him anyway, it only makes sense to move closer to him."

"I can't think about making changes until I solve the case I'm working on," Will replied.

"How's that coming along?"

There was a momentary pause followed by a disgusted snort. "It's *not*."

"Really," Madeline answered sympathetically. "Would you care to talk about it?"

"No. Let's change the subject to something more pleasant."

I walked into the living room. "Lunch is ready."

"Wonderful!" Madeline handed me her empty glass. "I'm starving."

They followed me into the dining room. Will held Madeline's chair for her as I walked into the kitchen and retrieved their plates. I'd made the sandwiches Madeline had requested, along with a cucumber salad and baked macaroni.

I went into the kitchen just as Daniel arrived and already had a plate prepared for him to eat at his favorite spot on the back step.

"Speaking of lighter subjects," Madeline said warmly to Will as I walked back into the dining room with a pitcher of ice water to refill their glasses, "Gloria sends her regards."

Will ignored her statement and busied himself putting a forkful of macaroni into his mouth.

"She misses you, Will. Why have you been avoiding her? You're breaking her heart."

"We're friends and that's all we were meant to be. I decided it was best to end our relationship before things got serious." He shrugged. "Gloria is a good woman, but she's not the one for me."

"I think she's perfect for you," Madeline stated in a sulking voice. "The way you're going, you're never going to find anyone."

"Maybe I don't want to find anyone. Maybe the right woman will find *me*."

I left the dining room wondering what kind of woman the *right one* would be and whether he'd know it when he saw her.

"Just because one woman cheated on you, that's no reason to be wary of all females," Madeline cajoled.

A stony silence ….

"Will!"

"I'm not wary of all women. I like 'em as much as the next guy, but I'm not in the market for a wife right now, so just drop it, okay?"

Their conversation ceased as I prepared the dessert. When they finished their lunch, I removed their plates and offered them coffee. They accepted and I slipped back into the kitchen to retrieve the coffee pot.

"Say, I have the pictures from the party," Madeline said to Will as I poured her coffee. "Do you want to see them?" At Will's reply, she snatched her purse off the table and pulled out a stack of finished photos. "Here. My new camera did an excellent job."

Back in the kitchen, I sliced pie-shaped wedges of warm pineapple skillet cake. I brought out their dessert and smiled gratefully at the delighted response I received from Madeline. It had been my first try at making this cake and it had turned out beautifully.

Will sifted through his sister's photographs, smiling, as I set his dessert in front of him. When I returned to the kitchen, I heard him say, "May I keep this one?"

"Of course," Madeline replied. "Take as many as you like. I can always get more printed."

I got busy cleaning up the kitchen and made so much noise I didn't hear any more of their conversation until Madeline practically shouted, "Will! Are you listening to me?"

His chair slid back, scraping across the wood floor. "Sorry, Maddie, but I've got to get back to work." He went into the parlor and shuffled papers for a minute then grabbed his hat and keys.

"Where are you going?" Madeline pushed her chair back, sounding frustrated. "I thought we were—"

"I need to check on something important," he said hastily. "Thanks for coming over for lunch, Maddie. I'll call you tomorrow."

He tipped his hat to me as he walked through the kitchen on his way to the back door. "I'll see you later," he said briskly. I'd worked for him long enough now to know what that meant.

Don't wait up for me...

Chapter Nine

"Clean up these newspapers," Louisa said to me on Tuesday morning in her usual snappish way. Will had just left the house and we were alone for the rest of her shift. "Will wants them all removed from the top of this file cabinet today."

He'd probably asked her to do it, but of course, her pride wouldn't allow her to stoop so low as to carry out such a menial housekeeping task. Not when she had me to boss around. With my hands perched on my hips, I glared at her. "*Please*," I said, "*please* clean up these newspapers."

"Just *do* it!"

I'd become tired of her constant harping at me to perform my duties. In fact, I was just tired today. Period. And in no mood to put up with her imperiousness. "Look, I don't work for you, Louisa, and I never did. We're equal. You need to stop ordering me around."

She turned her back to me and sat down at her typewriter. "I don't consider myself on the same level as domestic help." She turned her head. "And Will doesn't either. He told me I was extraordinary."

Knowing what I knew now about Will's past, his penchant for glamorous blondes, and his disinterest in settling down, I had a mind to inform Louisa that her romantic plans for him were merely all in her head—and not in his. Even so, she had to know in her heart he would never give her a second thought, except as his extraordinary secretary. And she had to know that I knew it too.

Realizing I was becoming as petty as she was, I mentally shook it off and grabbed the stack of papers. On the way to the kitchen, the papers shifted in my arms and spilled all over the floor. Irritated, I gathered them up, but one section came apart in my hands and sailed across the room. I dumped the stack on the counter, walked over to it, and snatched it off the floor. An article toward the bottom of the page caught my eye. Curious, I sat down and read a story about a place in St. Paul at the corner of Minnehaha Avenue and Chatsworth Street run by nuns for homeless, wayward, and criminal girls—The House of the Good Shepherd. Suddenly I knew I'd found the place to have my baby. Life at this institution would be cloistered, thread-bare, and filled with rules, but was I not used to that? Growing up in Swede Hollow, my family had no electricity or running water and as a kid, I never left the confines of our little shanty town except to attend public school.

Unlike Mamma's house, Gus would never think to look for me there.

The more I stared at the article, the more convinced I became that going to this place was the right move for me. Sadly, though, I had no one to talk to about it and it made me feel truly alone. Daniel was the only one in Will's house who knew of my condition...

I walked into the pantry and opened the basement door. "Daniel? Are you down there?" No one answered. I started to shut the door but halfway, I paused. I'd never gone down to his living quarters, not even to clean and I wondered what the place looked like. Perhaps he was working in a back room and couldn't hear me.

I opened the door all the way and stepped gingerly down the steep, narrow stairway to look for him. At the bottom of the staircase, I looked around in surprise. Daniel's apartment consisted of one large room with a bed, a sofa, and a small table with two chairs. Against one wall, he'd built a long workbench. Daylight shone through the narrow windows located near the ceiling, but not enough to adequately light the room.

The rapid tap-tap-tap of Louisa's typing echoed through the basement almost as loudly as if I were standing next to her. *That's odd*, I thought. The noise seemed to vibrate through the floor.

Puzzled, I walked across the room and looked upward. Someone had cut a rectangular opening in the ceiling under the radiator and placed a grate over it. My jaw dropped. Daniel could hear every word spoken in the parlor! I wondered if he'd done that to spy on Will or if he'd cut the hole to monitor Will's clients for security reasons.

Someone walked by the window. I only saw a pair of overall-clad legs, but the idea that Daniel might catch me snooping around his apartment prompted me to race back up the stairs and quickly shut the door. I waited for him to walk into the kitchen, but he didn't appear.

After that, I got busy cleaning Will's bedroom and bathroom until it was time to make Daniel's lunch. I made him another sandwich and heated the rest of the baked macaroni, adding a little cheese to the top to moisten it. He appeared in the kitchen right at noon.

I served him lunch and went out on the back step to sit with him while he ate. I showed him the newspaper and told him of my plans.

"Don't do this," he begged me. "The Good Shepherd Home isn't the place for you. I'll admit, I don't know how you got into your…situation, but you're neither wayward nor a criminal."

Though he meant well, he didn't realize what he was asking. Since he didn't know the whole story, I had a difficult time convincing him I had no other choice.

"Let me take care of you," he said with urgency in his voice. "I'll get a better place for us and a new job that pays more. You won't have to worry about anything."

Oh my gosh…

I stood, extremely uncomfortable with this conversation, and wished wholeheartedly that I'd kept my big mouth shut. "I've got to get back to work," I said in a rush and placed my hand on his shoulder. "We'll talk about it again later."

I went into the house and pounded my fists at my sides, angry with myself for carelessly opening a door that would be difficult to shut. What was I thinking?

I wasn't thinking—either time I divulged personal information to him. That's the problem.

Vowing to myself to straighten out the situation with Daniel— when Louisa wasn't around—I went back upstairs and immersed myself in my work.

* * *

I didn't see Daniel for the rest of the day. Later that evening, I had a bite to eat and went up to my room to lay down and enjoy one of my favorite pastimes—completing the daily crossword puzzle in the newspaper. The stack of newspapers I'd taken from the parlor sat piled on my dresser. I'd turned on my lamp and started to browse through the first one when the doorbell rang.

"Who on earth could that be this time of night," I grumbled to myself as I rose from the bed. I slipped on my shoes.

The doorbell rang again as I hurried down the front stairs. I peered through the sheer curtains in the alcove to see who it was, and to my surprise, Madeline and Gloria stood on the porch, waiting for me to let them in. I hurried to the door and opened it.

"Esther, is Will home?" Madeline breezed past me with Gloria on her heels. "I'd have let myself in, but you had the screen door locked."

Ever since Gus and his bodyguards had invaded the porch waiting for Will, I'd begun locking all of the doors at night.

"No, I'm afraid he's not here." I still had my uniform on, minus the apron, and stood with my hands clasped. "He left early this morning and hasn't been back."

"He must still be working on his missing person case." Madeline grimaced. "He's really obsessed with finding that woman."

Sweat began to form on my upper lip, but it didn't have anything to do with the summer heat.

Madeline smiled at Gloria. "Well, since we're here now, we'll just hang around for a little while to see if he shows up." She ushered Gloria into the living room. "Esther, bring us something to drink." She winked at me, letting me know she meant something stronger than water, preferably illegal.

"Yes, ma'am," I said and went to fetch the bottle of whiskey Will always kept in his bottom desk drawer. I found two bottles, one half-empty and one unopened. I pulled out the half-empty one and took it into the living room. Madeline already had the Victrola credenza open and was looking through a stack of records. While they were picking out their favorite songs, I fetched a couple of crystal lowball glasses and filled the ice bucket with ice from the Frigidaire.

They ended up entertaining themselves for hours, waiting for Will to return. The women drained the bottle of whiskey and devoured both a plate of chicken salad with lettuce on toast squares and a couple of pieces of pie.

At midnight, I found both women asleep, each one draped over an overstuffed arm of the sofa. I turned off the Victrola and dimmed the lights, wondering what to do. I certainly couldn't leave them alone like that. What if one of them got sick?

After placing a full glass of ice water on the parlor table for myself, I curled up in a wing chair and relaxed, listening to the sound of the crickets singing through the open window.

The next thing I knew, I was opening my eyes to find Will leaning over me. "Hey," he murmured in my ear, "what's going on here?"

"Oh..." Still in a groggy haze, I stretched out my legs and jumped out of the chair—and fell against him when my knees promptly buckled.

"Whoa," he said, catching me before I hit the floor. "Take it easy." His large hands, gentle yet strong, pressed against my waist and in one smooth motion, set me back on my feet as though I were as light as a feather. I placed my hands on his arms to steady myself and looked up. As his blue eyes searched mine, I had the feeling he had something else on his mind but was holding back. He pulled away as if reading my thoughts. His brows furrowed. "Have you been drinking too?"

"No, I'm—I'm just really tired. Someone had to stay with them. They've had too much to drink."

He gently let go of me and looked around. "I can see that. They look absolutely sozzled. Where'd they get the liquor?"

The insinuation in his voice prompted me to clasp my hands together and stare at the ceiling. "Ah..."

Will picked up the empty whiskey bottle stuck between two davenport cushions. "Did you give them this?"

"Miss Madeline told me to get it for her. At least I didn't give her the full one."

"H-m-m-m..."

"They showed up at about eight o'clock looking for you. I told them I didn't know when you'd be home, but they insisted on waiting."

"What did they want?"

"Miss Gloria wanted to talk to you." Well, that was her plan for the beginning of the evening anyway. No way was I going to divulge their grand scheme to loosen him up with whiskey so Gloria could seduce him. She was desperate to convince him they were meant for each other. Maybe so, but I had no reason to get involved. Not unless I wanted to start trouble on multiple fronts—which I surely didn't.

Will swept back the panels of his coat and put his hands on his hips. "I should have known something was up when Maddie began preaching to me yesterday at lunch. Lord knows what else these two had up their sleeves tonight, but I've got a good idea. Were you in on this little matchmaking trap, too?"

"Me?" Shocked that he would think me willing to collude with his sister, I vigorously shook my head. "I'm just the housekeeper."

He gave me a dubious look. "I'll get Daniel to help me take them home."

I opened my mouth to argue why they should stay but he cut me off—

"Wake them up and get them ready to go by the time I get back." He started walking toward the kitchen. "That's an *order*."

Okay, Mr. Grouchy.

I had no luck rousing either woman. When Will reappeared with Daniel, they had to carry Madeline and Gloria out to Madeline's sedan. Will planned to drive her car to her apartment and Daniel would follow in the Chrysler.

I trailed them out to the curb and waited until they'd placed the women, now half-awake and grumbling, safely in the back seat. "Here are their handbags." I opened the front passenger door and set them on the seat.

"Thanks," Will said as he tucked Gloria's foot inside the car and shut the back door. Silvery rays from the front porch light cast enough light to see his face. His anger had ebbed and the disciplined, confident manner of the man I knew was back. "You were right to watch over the girls," he said, "but I can see it's been a long day for you. You look completely exhausted and the last thing I want is for you to get sick. Don't clean up. You can do it tomorrow at your leisure. Go straight to bed. Understand?"

"Okay, thank you," I replied wearily and turned to trudge back to the house.

"Hey." He caught me by the arm, gently turning me around. "I want you to sleep late tomorrow morning. You've earned it. I'll make my own breakfast."

I thanked him again and walked back to the house, so tired I could barely think. Still, I wondered, was he acting extraordinarily generous, or did I really look that bad? Either way, I planned to take him up on his offer. These late nights were becoming too much for me to handle.

*   *   *

The next morning, I came downstairs just as Louisa arrived. I must have looked disheveled by the way her gaze swept over me in disapproval. I'd gone straight to bed and neglected to rinse out my uniform, but it wasn't soiled so I put it back on for one more day. As tired and grumpy as I was, I didn't care one way or the other.

I spent a few minutes in the kitchen, drinking coffee and munching toast with strawberry-rhubarb jelly. Will and Daniel had helped themselves to a big pan of caramel-pecan rolls I'd made yesterday, leaving crumbs all over the counter. I ignored the mess and sat down, hoping I felt better as the day wore on.

Daniel must have heard my feet patter on the kitchen floor. He came up from the basement carrying his coffee cup and walked straight toward me. "How are you feeling?"

"I'm fine. Just tired today. As you know, I was up quite late last night."

He nodded with understanding, but his green eyes mirrored deep concern. "Take it easy today. Don't push yourself, okay? Let me know if you need help."

"Okay, thanks. Don't worry, I don't have any choice. I'm moving pretty slow right now, but I'll catch up on sleep tonight."

He gave me a quick hug and helped himself to a fresh cup of coffee.

"Have another caramel roll."

Smiling, he grabbed one and headed outside.

After a cup of coffee and sufficient time to clear my head, I went into the living room to clean up the mess from last night. The snack plate I'd prepared still lay in the center of the parlor table. Two dried-up pieces of toast and shriveled lettuce were all that remained. Someone had eaten the chicken salad and discarded the rest. The top of the Victor credenza stood open and records—some still in their paper jackets and some not—were strewn about the room. I removed the snack plate right away and began to pick up the records to organize them and put them away.

Will had brought in some empty wooden crates from his car and had instructed Louisa to purge all of the files from his file cabinets, claiming it was time to store all of his old, closed cases. The files had been organized by year, but now he wanted them alphabetized for easier access.

Louisa surveyed the crates then cast a sly look at me.

Oh, no. You're not commandeering me for that job...

I turned around and kept working in the living room, feeling her gaze burn through my back. She was dying to know who'd been partying in Will's house last night, but I had no intention of telling her. What went on in Will's private life was his business and not mine to divulge— especially to her.

My foot hit something under the parlor table. I bent down and found a lowball glass full of liquid. Some of it had sloshed over the side of the glass onto the rug. I picked up the glass and sniffed it, wondering whether it was plain water or contained some whiskey—in which case I'd have to scrub it out of the rug instead of merely blotting it with a rag. To my dismay, it had a strong odor, suggesting it was part liquor.

"What are you doing?"

I turned around to find Louisa glaring suspiciously at me.

"What's in your hand?"

I absolutely did not have the patience for her theatrics today. I shoved the glass behind my back. "None of your business. Don't you have files to pack?"

Louisa whirled around. "Will! Esther is drinking on the job!"

"What?" Will flipped through a file on his desk, preoccupied with its contents. "What are you talking about?"

"I saw her. Just now. Drinking a glass of liquor." Louisa pointed at me. "She still has it in her hand!"

Will looked up and gave me a baffled look. "Esther? What's going on?"

Louisa walked toward me and snatched away the glass. "See?" Holding it close to her face, she sniffed it and grimaced. "Ewww... It's liquor all right. She's drinking whiskey right under your nose!"

I rolled my eyes wishing I could slap that sneer right off her face, but even if I had the opportunity, I didn't have the energy. "I don't drink." At least, I hadn't since I'd become pregnant. I couldn't stand even the smell of the stuff anymore. "I found it under the table." I stepped forward and pointed at the red lipstick clinging to the rim of the glass. "See that? It's proof that it belonged either to Miss Madeline or to your *girlfriend*, Miss Gloria."

Checkmate.

I didn't look at Louisa, but I could almost hear her jaw drop. With perverse satisfaction, I raised my brows to let Will know I'd had enough of this ridiculous, malicious bickering.

Obviously, Will did, too. Placing his palms on his desk, he stood up and leaned forward staring with annoyance at both of us. "Do I have to separate you two? Because if I do—"

"No." I picked up my cleaning rag. "I'm going into the kitchen and stay there for the rest of the morning."

"Please do!" Louisa snapped in an effort to get the last word. Not this time.

"Oh, shut up!" I stomped into the kitchen and stuffed a huge piece of caramel roll into my mouth. After that, I flounced out the back door and sat on the step, steaming, but at the same time, extremely embarrassed over the childish way I'd just acted. That wasn't like me. Something had to give here. Will had an extraordinary secretary and an extraordinary housekeeper but the two were like oil and water—or more appropriately like sweet and sour. Except that I was becoming more like her every day—as sour as a green apple in July.

Once I cooled down, I went back into the kitchen to clean up and bake a cake, lining the bottom of the pan with butter, sugar, strawberries, and rhubarb—or pie plant, as my mother called it. Will's mother had grown a huge plant in the backyard and I'd been cutting it for cooking and baking all summer.

The thought of baking a new cake calmed me and diverted my mind away from the ugly, tense situation in the other room. I went to work and put it together, humming a tune I'd heard on Mamma's favorite radio music program. While it baked, the house was filled with a wonderful aroma.

About mid-morning, Will came into the kitchen for a fresh cup of coffee. "Something in here really smells good." He grinned, apparently having forgiven me for my unbecoming tantrum. "Whatever you're doing, keep it up because it's making my mouth water."

I smiled sweetly and showed him the cake cooling on a wire rack. "I'll cut you a piece for dessert after lunch."

He filled his cup and turned to me. "Don't bother making me anything. I'm going downtown for a lunch meeting with Peter Garrett." He checked his pocket watch. "I'll probably leave in a couple of minutes."

I nodded silently, relieved I didn't need to make a noonday meal. I had ample leftovers to heat up for Daniel.

On his way out of the kitchen, Will tugged on my apron strings. He began to chuckle when the bow came apart and the strings fell to my sides.

"Hey!" I whispered, but at the same time, I couldn't help laughing.

Fifteen minutes later, Will grabbed his hat. "See you later," he said to Louisa. He walked into the kitchen and tipped his hat as he passed through. "See you later, Esther."

At noon, Louisa went home. I made Daniel's lunch and went upstairs to my room to take a desperately needed nap.

*   *   *

A sharp noise downstairs awoke me after dark. The clock on my wall read nine o'clock in the evening. Had I really slept this long?

I stood up and looked out the window. There were several cars parked along the street but I didn't recognize any of them. Had Madeline and Gloria come back to the house in Gloria's car this time to slip a matrimonial noose around Will's neck?

Curious, I put on my summer robe and quietly descended the back staircases until I'd reached the kitchen. As I tiptoed through the dark, I strained to hear voices in the front rooms, but the house was silent.

My mind began to spin. Was there a burglar in the house? Or could it be Gus? He'd given Will until tomorrow, Wednesday, to present a conclusion on this case. Was he sitting in the parlor, impatiently waiting for Will to come home and tell him tonight?

Looking through the kitchen doorway, I could tell there were only two lights on downstairs, the foyer lamp and a lamp in the front parlor. I moved stealthily into the dining room until I could peer through the wide doorways of the living room to see into the parlor.

Will sat at his desk with an open case file in front of him. A bottle of bootleg whiskey stood to his right. With a drink in his hand, he stared hard at something in the file, concentrating on it as though it greatly troubled him.

I wondered what he was studying; a document of some sort or a typed page filled with his own notes? From this distance, I couldn't tell, but I instinctively knew whatever he sat there trying to make sense of must be connected to my missing person case. Tomorrow he would stand in front of Gus and report his findings. Would Gus be pleased or more upset than ever over my disappearance? I was certain I already knew the answer.

In a sudden burst of frustration, Will tossed back his whiskey in one gulp and slammed the empty glass on his desk. His left hand swept the file off the desk so rapidly I barely realized what he had done before the papers began to scatter to the floor like fallen leaves. Muttering a string of cuss words, he rested his elbows on his desk and buried his face in his hands.

His action stunned me. I didn't know what tomorrow would bring, but I had a feeling my life would never be the same again.

Chapter Ten

Something was amiss.

I sensed it the moment I woke up the next morning. Through my window, the leaden sky cast a dark pall over the neighborhood. The temperature and humidity had slowly risen through the night to the point where simply breathing had become uncomfortable. Everything I touched, including my shoes, had a sticky, moisture-saturated surface.

My clean uniform hung on a hanger in my bathroom, but when I put it on, I found the fabric hadn't completely dried. Since it was too hot to wear my nighttime uniform with long sleeves, I had to wear the damp one with the hope it would eventually dry on my body.

The situation proved no less comfortable when I went downstairs to make coffee and start breakfast. Will came downstairs at seven o'clock, wearing a white shirt, open at the neck with the sleeves rolled up to his elbows. He barely said a word to me. I set the food on the table in front of him. He consumed it in brooding silence.

He has to give Gus his final determination—today. No wonder he's unhappy. I wouldn't want to be the bearer of bad news to that man, either...

I went into the living room to place a pan of ice in front of the fan and noticed Will had cleaned up the scattered mess of paper in his office sometime last night. The manila file folder once again sat in the center of his desk. The liquor bottle and glass were gone.

Louisa appeared at eight o'clock carrying a black umbrella, the lines around her mouth more taut than usual. She, too, sensed the oppressive mood pervading the house. She resumed her task of reorganizing Will's closed cases to be stored in wooden crates for transport into storage. It took the entire morning to go through the remaining files, straighten the papers inside and list the case name on the folder tab with a bold pen. Stacks of folders were spread across the floor in alphabetical order.

Except for the parlor, I spent the morning dusting and cleaning all the rooms and staircases downstairs. I didn't know if my sudden burst of energy was due to the excessive amount of sleep I'd received yesterday or if the tension rolling off my employer had made me so nervous I had to keep moving, but I didn't stop until an unsettling incident stopped *me*.

Around noon, I stood in the kitchen finishing my lunch preparations when I heard Will tell Louisa to close the parlor doors. Obviously, he had something to say to her that he wanted to keep private, but shutting up the room didn't dampen my determination to find out what it was. The mere fact that he wanted to be alone with her when he talked to her caused a tinge of foreboding I couldn't quell.

Fortunately for me, the sliding wooden doors dividing the parlor from the living room didn't quite shut, leaving me a blessed sliver of space with which to watch the private goings-on. I removed my shoes and tiptoed in my stocking feet through the living room to the doors and peered through the crack.

Will stood in front of his desk. "Sit down, Louisa."

Her hands shook as she smoothed out her skirt to sit in the chair facing him. From behind, her long black dress and brown hair wound into a tight bun made her look like an older spinster than she was. Even with her back to me, I could sense her uncertainty. I'd never seen her so anxious or vulnerable. "Did I do something wrong?"

"No," Will replied as he leaned against his wooden desk, "you've always performed your job with extraordinary excellence. I appreciate everything you've done to keep me organized and to turn out your best work." His hands gripped the edge of the desk. "But unfortunately, I'm shutting down this office and won't need your help any longer."

I blinked. He...*what*? I leaned closer to the door to watch the scene unfold.

Louisa's pale, slender hands clutched her throat. "Are you telling me you're going out of business? But...why? You've had plenty of clients since I started working for you."

"I'm not going out of business. Rather, I'm moving my agency downtown St. Paul to the Endicott Building. Yesterday, I signed a contract with an attorney by the name of Peter Garrett to take over half of his office space. It wasn't a good idea to run my business out of my private residence. After what happened with Gus LeDoux, surely you can understand why I've found it necessary to make these changes."

"You'll need a secretary! I'll take the streetcar downtown every day to work. My house is only a block from the main route."

Will shook his head. "Peter already has a secretary who'll work for both of us so it's not possible." He reached into his pocket and pulled out an envelope. "Here are your wages for the entire week and a written reference." He held it out. "This is the end of your employment with me."

Louisa jumped from her chair, ignoring his extended hand. "But, Will, you said I was extraordinary! How can you do this to me?" She splayed her hands on his chest. Her tearful voice trembled. "You led me to believe you cared about me."

Will dropped the envelope on his desk. "Listen to me," he said firmly as he gently placed his hands on her forearms, holding her at an arm's length. "I don't know why you've come to the conclusion I had romantic feelings for you, but it's not true. I've never given you any indication that my regard for you amounted to more than professional courtesy and respect. You're my secretary, Louisa, nothing more."

"What about my reputation? My mother thinks—"

"Your mother's opinion doesn't concern me." He let go of her and walked behind his desk as if to put more than just emotional distance between them. "I've noted in my reference that your professional skills are excellent. You shouldn't have any trouble finding another job."

"When my family finds out you've jilted me, I'll be ruined—"

"Goodbye, Louisa. I wish you well."

At first, she stood riveted in place, frozen like a statue. Then, as if his words had finally sunk in, she snatched the envelope and threw it at his chest. Without a word, she picked up her small handbag, pulled open the sliding doors, and promptly left the house. The screen door banged shut behind her.

Shocked and amazed, I gazed through the crack, watching Will stare in the direction Louisa had gone with an unreadable expression on his face. After a moment, he sat down with a heavy sigh and raked his hands through his hair. I had the feeling he'd expected some resistance from her, but nothing on the scale of what he'd received. He reached down, pulled open a drawer, and took out his whiskey bottle and glass.

I turned around and stepped softly to the kitchen. Daniel stood at the counter, waiting for me, his solemn gaze meeting mine. "So, he finally let her go, huh? It's about time."

He probably heard the entire exchange downstairs, I thought and nodded. "Do you think I'll be next?"

He frowned. "Why do you say that?"

I picked up a kitchen towel and through force of habit, wiped imaginary dishwater off my hands. "I don't know. It just feels like there's more to come."

"Ah," he said with a dismissive wave of his hand. "The man's gotta eat and he sure doesn't know the first thing about cooking." He grinned. "Neither do I. I'm pretty sure your job is safe."

I pulled a plate out of the cabinet to dish up his lunch, but he halted me by resting his hand on my forearm. "Have you given any thought to our discussion, Esther?"

I glanced at him but didn't answer.

"I mean it. I'll get a place for us so you don't have to go to a home for prostitutes."

"No, I haven't decided yet." Truth was, I had thought about it for one second and knew it was the worst possible choice I could make. It would not only endanger both of our lives but would give Daniel false hopes about a future with me. I simply didn't know how to break the sad truth to him.

He looked disappointed. "Okay, but you've got to make up your mind soon."

"I will. I promise."

I dished up his plate, including his dessert, and sent him downstairs, where it was measurably cooler, to eat his lunch.

Instead of calling Will to the dining room, I made up a plate for him and took it to him in the parlor. It was cooler in there than in the dining room. He was still sitting at his desk when I walked through the foyer and into the room with his food.

"Here's your lunch." Pushing his folder aside, I set both the main plate and the dessert plate in front of him and walked away.

"Hey, c'mon back."

I stopped in my tracks and turned around.

"Sit down for a couple of minutes and visit with me while I eat."

"Okay," I said tentatively and sat in the chair Louisa used to occupy.

"These ribs are mouth-watering," he said as he dug into the short ribs I'd spent several hours slowly cooking for him. The meat literally fell off the bones when he picked them up with his fork.

I smiled, hoping that meant my future was secure, at least for a little while longer. "I'm glad you like them."

We talked about safe subjects, like the muggy heat, the impending storm predicted for later this afternoon, and what he wanted me to make for lunch tomorrow, purposely avoiding any reference to the last conversation he'd had in this room. Even so, he had to have known I'd heard every word.

Will finished his cake and pushed the plate across his desk. "That was terrific but really sweet."

I sprang from the chair and grabbed the dirty dishes. "I forgot to bring you some coffee. It's a bit sweltering for a hot beverage, but would you like a cup anyway?"

"Okay," he replied enthusiastically. "I could use some good coffee. Oh, and bring me a glass of ice water, too. Okay, *Char*?"

"Sure, I'll be right back…"

I slowly turned around.

Our gazes met and suddenly I realized what I'd done. I looked into the eyes of the man who literally held my life in his hands and knew the game was over.

I had lost.

*　*　*

At first, neither of us spoke. As the enormity of his discovery sunk in, a surge of hopelessness and defeat swept over me like a swell in a storm.

"Shut the doors," he said to me. "We need to talk."

My first response was to run away, but I knew that would be a fruitless effort. Will would catch me before I reached the kitchen. Instead, I set the dishes on the parlor table in the foyer and pulled the doors shut then walked back to his desk, deciding to confess all and get it over with. "How long have you known the truth about me?"

"Not long," he said quietly. "Two days."

That surprised me. "How did you find out? Did my mother confess that she'd seen me alive after you put pressure on her?"

"No," he said defensively, "I'd never take advantage of a woman in her condition. It was something I stumbled upon completely by accident." He opened the file and pulled out a photograph; the one Madeline had given him on Monday during lunch. Handing it to me he said, "Take a look at this and tell me what you see—besides a woman who is definitely camera shy."

I gingerly accepted the photo and looked down at it.

Oh, dear God...

The black and white print was supposed to be a shot of one of Madeline's friends, but this was the one where she'd accidentally caught me in the background. In the picture, I'd looked straight at the camera. My wide-eyed fear of being in the photograph was unmistakable.

Will held out my wedding picture. "Now place this one next to it and compare the two."

I did as he'd asked and the two pictures were identical. Even with the red hair and glasses, no one could fail to see the same girl wore both the maid uniform and the bridal gown.

"Still," I argued, "there are a lot of people whose features are identical enough to be twins. Haven't you ever had someone mistake you for someone else?"

"Exactly," he said as he retrieved the photos and put them back in the file. "Mistaken identity happens all the time. So, I started to think backward and I remembered Maddie mentioning a couple of times how she had heard your voice before. She used to meet friends occasionally at La Coquette, so she had probably heard you speak at some point." He leaned forward. "As you pointed out, though, one coincidence isn't enough to build an airtight case."

"What other mistakes did I make?"

"Only one." He raised one brow. "After your husband's first visit, you called him Gus when we were discussing your re-employment. I remembered thinking at the time it was a little odd for you to refer to a man you'd never met by his first name. Later, however, it made sense when I realized who you really were. You were still pretty shaken that day from seeing him again and I imagine it just slipped out."

"You have no idea…" I took a deep breath and sat down. "What about when he saw me running away at my mother's house?"

"He didn't see your face so we couldn't be sure. I don't substitute hunches for the real thing, Char. I deal with verified facts."

I looked down and saw a copy of the newspaper article in his file that had my picture in the center. He'd drawn a pair of glasses on my face. "I guess the little facts eventually added up to a strong conclusion."

"Not really." Will stood up and walked around his desk, stopping right in front of me. I tensed, half-expecting him to slap a pair of handcuffs on me and drag me out to his car to turn me over to Gus.

"That was enough to get me started," Will continued, "but I had to have more concrete evidence than that." He leaned against the desk, seemingly in no hurry to apprehend me. "I went to Finnegan's Hotel and asked them if they had ever employed a young girl by the name of Esther Smith. They had never heard of her, but when I showed them the pictures of you, they verified that you had worked for them. However, they only knew you as Charlotte Johnson—the girl who'd quit to marry Gus LeDoux."

I pulled off my headband and nervously fiddled with the ruffled edges of the white fabric. "Is that where you went yesterday after your meeting?"

"No." He folded his arms. "I went to Swede Hollow and showed your pictures to a dozen people. Every person who knew you correctly identified you."

I glared at him stubbornly though I wanted to cry. "Why are you telling me all this? Are you trying to impress me with your cleverness?"

"I believe it is your right to know."

The magnitude of what was about to transpire in my life began to sink in. I gave him a pleading look. "What are you going to do with me?"

Reaching out, he gently pulled my glasses away from my face and set them aside. "I'm going to let you decide."

His answer confused me. "I don't understand."

"Look, Char, you're not Gus' property, even if he seems to think so," Will said tenderly as he grasped my chin with his thumb and forefinger, tilting my face upward. "You have a say in this, too. If you don't want to go back to him, just say the word and it won't happen. At least, not because of me. I'll never force you to return to him against your will. Tell me what you want to do."

I didn't need any time to think about my answer. "Escape. Again. I can't go back to that life." I looked down at my abdomen. "I need to disappear for my baby's sake *and* mine."

His eyes widened. "So, you really are…?"

I nodded. "About five and a half months."

He gazed at my abdomen, perplexed. "But...nothing shows..."

I placed my hands on the small of my back. "He's all back here, but I *am* starting to get a small tummy."

Will cleared his throat. "I'll take your word for it." He pushed himself away from the desk and took my hands in his, pulling me to my feet. He looked deeply into my eyes. "As much as I want to keep you here, I have to find another place for you to stay. When I tell Gus I can't locate you, he's going to go crazy and who knows what he'll do. You need to be far away from this house at that time."

Suddenly, the room began to spin.

"Char, what's the matter?" Will slipped his arm around my waist and steadied me. "Are you all right? Your face is flushed."

Gripping my arms around him, I rested my cheek against his broad chest. "With the doors closed, this room is like an oven. I need to get off my feet."

He gently lowered me back down on the chair. "You should drink some cool water. I'll be right back." He shoved open the doors to the living room and walked swiftly to the kitchen. Immediately, the fan in the living room poured a welcome breeze in my direction.

The dizziness had subsided by the time he returned with the water. Lowering to one knee, he placed the glass to my lips. "Is that better?"

I nodded.

"Good." He stood. "I think you need to lie down and rest. I'll get a pillow for you to stretch out on the davenport in front of the fan."

"No," I argued. "I'd rather go upstairs and change clothes instead. I need to exchange this hot uniform for something less restricting. I'll feel a lot better after I do that."

"Whatever you say. Do you need help getting up the stairs?"

131

"No, I can make it by myself."

He looked concerned. "Are you sure?"

"Yes, I'll be fine."

Will walked over to the other set of doors and pulled them open. "I have to go out and I don't want you in harm's way if Gus decides to show up here instead of his lawyer's office."

The thought frightened me. "Where are you going?"

He grabbed his hat off the coat tree and turned around. "To find a place for you to stay until we can arrange something permanent. I won't be gone long. Go upstairs, pack your bag, and wait for me. *Do it now.*"

"Gladly." I stood up, getting my bearings as he swiftly walked to the kitchen and left by the back door.

I only got as far as the stairs. The moment I placed my hand on the newel post, Louisa stepped out of the alcove and onto the landing, her forgotten umbrella in her hand. The sly, vindictive look in her eyes left no doubt she'd heard every word of the conversation.

And she was about to expose me.

*   *   *

I grit my teeth at her knowing smile. "How long have you been hiding in the alcove, spying on us?"

Louisa stepped down from the landing, standing face to face with me. "Not long. I heard most of it outside on the porch. You shut the doors, but you neglected to shut the windows. I had a ringside seat to your touching little performance."

Gripping the newel post for support, I steadied myself. "What do you want?"

Her eyes narrowed. "I want you gone from this house. *Forever.* Everything was fine until you wiggled your way in here, causing a rift between Will and me!"

You did that yourself, Miss Amundsen, with no help from the housekeeper.

I laughed in her face, though I didn't find the situation a bit funny. This woman had major emotional issues that had nothing to do with neither Will nor me and I wondered what had happened in her past to make her so delusional. "I had nothing to do with Will's decision to move his business and let you go. It was his sister, Madeline, who convinced him to make the change."

"I don't believe you," Louisa spat. "You manipulated him! Now I know you've been deceiving him all along because you needed a place to hide from your criminal of a husband."

"That's not true! I never expected to involve Will, but when Gus showed up one day—"

"Yes, you did!" Louisa screamed. "You're nothing but a lying little schemer. I've seen the way Will looks at you in your short, little day dress. You're alone with him in this house every night. Do you think I don't know what's going on? A man only wants a doxy like you for *one thing.*"

"A man only wants a spinster like you to type his notes," I fired off before I realized what I'd said.

With tears in her eyes, Louisa raised her umbrella, threatening to strike me with it.

Try it sister, and it'll be the last time...

Pregnant or not, I possessed twice the strength she had. Growing up in Swede Hollow had taught me how to defend myself against bullies. With one shove, I could knock her through the screen door and onto her backside on the porch so fast she'd never know what hit her. I could, but I'd never do it. Violence was Gus' way—not mine.

"Look," I said quietly, "it's time for you to leave, Louisa. This conversation is pointless. Your quarrel is with Will, not me. Even so, you need to accept his right to conduct his affairs as he sees fit and get on with your life."

"As soon as you're gone, I will. Once I have him all to myself again, he'll realize how much he misses me." She tossed her umbrella then walked into the parlor and pulled out the top drawer of her desk, selecting a small piece of paper. Whirling around, she set the paper on the desktop, picked up Will's phone, and waited for the operator.

Sweat began to bead on my upper lip. "What are you doing?"

She gave me a haughty look. "Getting rid of you."

Realizing what that meant, I walked swiftly to her and tried to pull the phone out of her hands, but as soon as I reached her, she spun away, turning her back to me.

Louisa recited the number when the operator came on the line.

"Give me that phone!" Furious, I reached around her and tried to pull the telephone away from her again, but she picked up my water glass and whirled toward me, throwing cold water in my face.

The sudden *swoosh* of icy moisture in my eyes momentarily distracted me, but the delay bought Louisa enough time to cause the greatest amount of damage she could ever do to me.

"Hello, Mr. LeDoux? It's Miss Amundsen from Will Van Elsberg's office."

I released my grip on her, knowing it was too late to stop her now. Even if I were to end her call before she'd finished her little speech, Gus would try to call back and if he couldn't reach anyone, his suspicious mind would prompt him to jump in his car and race over here.

She shot me a triumphant, sideways glance. "Mr. Van Elsberg has your wife in custody and he's requesting you to take her off his hands as soon as possible. Yes, she's here at the house. Thank you. Goodbye."

Louisa hung up. "Your husband is on his way." She turned to me with a satisfied sneer. "Don't try to run this time. You won't get far." She looked me up and down. "Not in *your* condition."

With her head held high, Louisa strode out of the house.

Gasping for breath, I gripped the edge of Will's desk for support.

Well, Char, what did you expect? You knew this day would inevitably come. Now, what are you going to do?

I only had two options—leave right now and take my chances or face my husband and stand my ground. No matter which one I chose, the odds of surviving now were slim to none.

With a tired sigh, I leaned against Will's desk and covered my eyes with the palms of my hands, contemplating my next move. One thing was certain, I could no longer run away from who I was.

It was time to stand my ground and let the chips fall...

Chapter Eleven

Not knowing how long it would take Gus to arrive, I ran upstairs to retrieve the pearl-handled revolver from my satchel but left my housekeeping uniform on. In all the time I'd owned the gun, I'd never once pulled the trigger. If the circumstances made it imperative for me to defend myself, could I do it now? Holding the heavy object in my hand, I remembered the warning Gus had given me in the past; if I pointed a weapon at someone, I'd better be ready to use it.

In my heart, I knew I couldn't fire it. I put it back in my bag and went downstairs.

Storms clouds rumbled overhead, turning the afternoon as dark as night. I'd stood in the foyer for what seemed like an eternity, though it couldn't have been more than ten minutes when a black car I'd never seen before slammed to a screeching halt at the curb. Before it came to a complete stop, the back door flew open and Gus jumped out. He strode purposefully toward the house with his bodyguards in tow, his hands clenched at his sides. The hard lines in his face were grim and unyielding. Any other man would have been beside himself with joy to find his long-lost wife, but Gus' tense stature portrayed a person facing the greatest crisis of his life.

So was I.

His shoes pounded out a steady tempo as he mounted the wooden steps and crossed the porch. The screen door opened, the wire spring on it stretching with an eerie whining sound. Lightning exploded overhead with an ear-splitting *crack*, sending a flash of brilliance across the sky as Gus' tall, imposing physique filled the doorframe. He entered taking slow, deliberate steps.

Our gazes locked, his stare boring into mine with a mixture of anger, shock, confusion, and hurt. I didn't know what outward impression my presence gave him, but inside my body, my heart pounded like a drumroll. My breathing quaked from the greatest emotional turmoil I'd ever known.

"You've been here all along," he said as his gaze swept over my uniform. He shook his head in disbelief. "Right under my nose."

I swallowed hard, trying to find my voice. "I answered an ad in the paper for a housekeeping job and got hired on the spot. But it—it was a coincidence. Will never knew—"

His gaze flicked toward the doorways behind me. "Where is Van Elsberg?"

"I have no idea," I said simply. "He went out."

Gus' chilling stare let me know he believed Will was purposely evading him—but as far as he was concerned, it wouldn't be for long. "Did you tell Sally Wentworth you were pregnant?"

"Yes, I did."

"You knew about it before the raid and you conveniently told others, but somehow you never found the time to tell me?" His fierce gaze intensified. "I want the truth, Char. Whose is it...mine...or his?"

Gus' assertion that I had been unfaithful with Will Van Elsberg floored me, but at the same time, it triggered emotions that had been festering ever since the night I'd caught him with Adrienne Devereaux. Fury over his gall to accuse me of his own misdeeds overrode my fear.

"How *dare* you suggest this child isn't yours!" I walked toward him, raising my chin in defiance, my finger jabbing him in the chest. "I wasn't concealing it from you. I'd just had it confirmed by the doctor that day and planned to tell you later when we were home alone. My news was too important to talk about at the club. I didn't want to be interrupted by people constantly banging on your office door to discuss business!" I jabbed him again, harder. "Don't you *ever* accuse me of that again, Gus LeDoux. You're the father and you know it!"

"Why should I believe you?" He pushed my hand away. "First, you disappear without a trace and you allow me to believe you're dead. Then I find out you're living with a guy who used to spend a lot of time at the club. *My* club." He grabbed both of my wrists and pulled my face close to his, forcing me to raise on my tiptoes. His eyes blazed. "Don't lie to me, Char," he threatened in a low, deadly voice. "All this time, he's been harboring you, and there can only be one reason why. You and Van Elsberg have been having an affair and laughing at me behind my back. When I get my hands on him, he's a *dead man!*"

"Stop it!" I screamed. "I never cheated on you. I *loved* you."

He glowered at me. "Then why did you leave me?"

Jerking my wrists from his grasp, I glared back with all the anger and injustice I could muster. "I gave you nine years of blind devotion. I even dutifully went along with your illegal activities. In the end, you repaid me by flaunting your mistress in my FACE." Swearing in French, I began to pummel his chest with my fists. "You betrayed *me*. I'm better off without you! Go back to your hideout and leave me alone!"

"I can't." His arms suddenly engulfed me, crushing me against his body as he forced his mouth upon mine. The raw emotion in his powerful kiss conveyed his desperation to save his marriage, but it was too late to rekindle what we once had. Too many issues had forced us apart. Our lack of trust in each other would forever keep us from the closeness we once had.

Gus ended the kiss and buried his face in my neck. "I've made mistakes, but things will change. I promise. I love you so much, Char. You're my weakness; my Achille's heel. Without you, I'm lost. Since you disappeared, I've been going crazy, not knowing whether you were alive or dead. Every night, I laid awake thinking about you—holding you in my arms, kissing you, feeling your soft body next to mine."

And all the while, you were lying next to your alluring mistress...

My heart went stone cold. "You will *never* change."

He lifted his head. "You're coming with me." He commanded me as though he hadn't heard a word I'd said.

"No!" I splayed my palms on his chest and tried to push him away. "You're a wanted man. It's not safe for me and the baby."

"I'm not letting you out of my sight ever again." He pinned me with a hard, unyielding stare. "W*e're leaving*, Char. Now, do as I say."

I backed away shaking my head. "Please, Gus, don't make me do this. I can't—"

"Let her go, LeDoux."

Surprised, I spun around to find Daniel and Will coming toward us from the back of the house. The knowing look in Daniel's eyes revealed he'd heard everything through the vent on the floor.

Gus pulled his Colt revolver from his shoulder holster and pointed it straight at Will's chest. "I wouldn't try to interfere if I were you, Van Elsberg. At this range, you don't stand a chance."

"The Feds are on their way," Will said in a steel-soft voice as the two men faced off. "Things could get ugly here in short order. Your wife is an innocent party. Don't drag her into your mess."

"Sirens, boss!" One of Gus' bodyguards yelled through the screen door. "We gotta go!"

"You're probably right, but I'm not leaving her with *you*," Gus said as he grabbed me by the arm and dragged me toward the door. One of his men opened it from the outside and I suddenly found myself standing on the porch. Once there, the situation escalated quickly.

Heavy thunder rumbled across the storm clouds swirling above the rooftops as sirens shrieked through the air. Gus' men jumped into their cars and used them to form a blockade at both ends of the block, from Dale Street to the Holcombe Circle at St. Alban's.

One of Gus' men handed him a submachine gun and told him Leonard was waiting for him in the car behind the brick building across the street.

"Cover me!" With an iron grip on my hand, Gus pulled me down the steps as gunfire erupted. I ran as fast as I could, panicking at the thought of getting shot and bleeding to death in the street. We managed to get across Laurel Avenue but did not slow down. The brick apartment building loomed ahead. Gus kept going until we crossed the small, curved lawn and slipped behind the building. A row of tall evergreen bushes hid us from sight as we made our way to the alley on the other side. But once we got there, Gus' car was nowhere in sight. He stopped in the center of the alley, gasping for breath and fervently looking around for his getaway vehicle.

Heavy footfalls pounded in rapid succession, coming from the sidewalk in front of the building. Gus went immediately into survival mode and pushed me to the ground. "Get down and stay there!"

I crouched on the flat surface with my legs folded under me, my hands covering my ears in anticipation of gunfire. When it came, the noise was so loud, so violent, I began to scream. My eyes were tightly closed, but in my mind's eye, I saw Albert lifting his Tommy Gun with both hands and killing a man in cold blood. "No, I can't," I cried with a sob. "I can't go through this again!"

When the shooting ended, Gus jerked me to my feet. "Come on, we've gotta go."

The acrid stench of gunpowder burned my nostrils. "No," I said hoarsely and struggled to get away. "This is madness, Gus! Can't you see that? We can't keep running. One day they'll catch up to us again and—"

"I said *move!*" He jerked me so hard, I stumbled, nearly falling to my knees.

"No," I cried as I fought him. "I'm not going anywhere with you. You're not the man I married, Gus. You're an *animal!*"

He grabbed me by the neck and jerked my face close to his as the thundering clouds rumbled non-stop. "This *animal* gave you everything! You had the life of a princess, but instead, you chose to take up with a two-bit gumshoe. If I can't have you, no one else will, either!"

I couldn't breathe. Dizziness began to overtake me. I pressed my hands against his chest to push him away, but Gus' arms were too strong. One of my hands slipped and landed against the butt of the pistol in his shoulder holster. Out of desperation, I grabbed the handle and pulled it out, leveling it at him with both hands, shaking uncontrollably.

Releasing his hand from my neck, he snorted at the ludicrousness of my bold move. "What do you think you're doing? Huh? Are you going to bump me off? You don't have the nerve." He curled his fingers around the barrel, but I stubbornly held on. "Let go of it, Char. Give me the gun."

I struggled with Gus to maintain my grip. It suddenly went off.

The submachine gun tucked under Gus' right arm dropped to his feet with a loud thump. His face registered shock as he slowly crumpled to the ground.

The pistol fell from my hands. I stood frozen, unable to comprehend what just happened. Until I saw the blood...

"Oh, dear God. What have I done," I cried and dropped to my knees, leaning over his lifeless body. Blood oozed from his gunshot wound, staining my apron and my hands. "Gus! Wake up!" I leaned over his chest and screamed in desperation. "Gus!"

Strong hands deftly lifted me to my feet. "There's nothing you can do for him now," a familiar deep voice whispered in my ear. "We have to take cover, Char. There's gunfire all around us. It's not safe here." Large raindrops began to splash on my face. Slipping into a daze, I didn't resist as Will's arm circled my waist. He lifted me off the ground and swiftly carried me away. As the alley disappeared from view, I numbly looked back and saw three bodies lying face-up on the ground. One belonged to my husband.

Gunfire erupted close by and the wail of more sirens, but it was the steady increase in the rain that prompted Will to stop at the side door of a garage and set me down. He tried the doorknob. Luckily, it opened— to an empty building. "We'll wait out the storm in here." He guided me inside and shut the door. "Hold still," he said in the dim light of a small window as he untied my blood-stained apron. With gentle hands, he peeled it off my body. He scrunched it into a tight ball and shoved it into the pocket of his jacket.

The rain began to downpour. It pounded on the roof, echoing a deep thrum in my ears. I let out a shaky breath. "What have I done…"

"It wasn't your fault. He was choking you," Will said softly and wrapped his arms around me, holding me close. "Don't blame yourself. You acted in self-defense."

Even so, despair wrenched my heart. I began to sob.

"It's going to be okay, sweetheart. I promise." Will placed the palm of his hand on the back of my head, pressing my face into his chest. "You're the strongest woman I've ever known. You're going to make it through this."

I slid my arms around him and cried all over his starched white shirt. Will rested his chin on the top of my head and silently rocked me as we stood in the wet, gray light, waiting for the storm to subside.

* * *

The rain stopped almost as quickly as it started. Will opened the door and stepped outside to ascertain if the coast was clear. The air was cool and damp. A steady stream of water dripped off the roof, splashing into the wooden rain barrel next to the garage. He dipped my arms into the barrel and washed the blood off them. "Come on," he said and took my hand.

We began to walk along St. Albans Street.

"After I get you away from here, I'm going back to the house to have a talk with the Feds," Will said gravely. "I'm going to tell them Gus forced you to leave with him. There are plenty of witnesses who saw him dragging you across the street to prove my claim that you weren't a willing participant and it gives credibility to the rest of my testimony. I'll say I followed you behind the building and saw him push you to the ground as agents came around the corner. One of the agents got off the first shot and hit Gus, but he managed to kill them both before he went down. I got you out of there before anyone could talk to you because of the gunfire and your medical condition."

"But, Will, I shot Gus with his own gun."

"One of the agents Gus shot had a Colt pistol like his and the guy died with the gun in his hand," Will said. "There wasn't any blood on the handle of Gus' gun so I slipped it back into his holster before I tended to you."

"It all happened so fast," I said, still somewhat dazed. "H-how could you notice so much detail and act so quickly in such a short time?"

"I'm a detective, Char. I'm trained for that."

He stopped and grabbed me by the shoulders. "Look, I'm trying to make this as easy for you as I can. You've been through enough as it is. When the Feds interview you, all you're going to say is that you didn't see anything because you were on the ground, fearing for your baby's life. My hope is, they'll be satisfied with that and leave you alone."

We traveled a couple of blocks, turning here and there until we came upon a long, one-story brick building on the corner of Dale Street and Grand Avenue. Will took me around to the back and stood at a plain wooden door.

"When we go inside, you stay right by me and don't say a word. Understand?"

I didn't understand, but I knew he had a good reason for his concern. I nodded.

"Take my arm."

I slipped my arm around his and waited as he knocked on the door. An eye peered through a small, square opening.

"Joe sent me," Will murmured.

The little opening closed and the big door was pulled ajar, a sign for us to enter. Will escorted me into a world I'd never seen, even at the club. For reasons I had never understood, Gus had forbidden me to step foot into any of the gambling rooms. Back then, I'd thrown a colossal fit over being barred from my own establishment. Now, with absolute clarity, I realized why.

The small, smoky room had dim lights hanging from the ceiling and a bar the length of one wall. The rest of the space was filled with gambling tables. Men of all sizes and shapes stood around the tables, drinking, playing cards, or throwing dice.

A small cheer suddenly erupted from a craps table in the back of the room.

It didn't take me long to realize I was the only woman in the place. And nearly everyone was staring at me because of it.

Will walked me to the bar, laid a silver dollar on the counter, and asked the bartender to call him a cab. The bartender glanced around, as though uncertain about his request then took the money and obliged.

Once the call went through, we left. I breathed a sigh of relief as the door shut behind us. I'd been in rough places before, but never anything like this.

Will walked me to the front of the building and pulled me into a covered doorway to get out of the steady drizzle that had begun as we waited for the cab to arrive. Several police cars sped down Dale Street. He pressed me farther into the doorway and filled the space with his body, providing cover for me as they passed by.

Fifteen interminable minutes later, the cab pulled up to the corner. We ran through the rain and Will quickly opened the door, guiding me inside.

"Where do you want to go?" he asked once he slid in next to me and shut the door. Water dripped from the brim of his Fedora. "You decide."

"Mamma's house," I replied without hesitation.

Will gave the east side address to the cabby and we drove away into the night.

Chapter Twelve

I stood at the graveside of my husband and struggled to keep my composure as the pallbearers lowered his casket into the ground. Hundreds of people were in attendance on the hot, sunny day at the sprawling grounds of Hillside Cemetery in Minneapolis. Gus' extended family made up a large group of mourners, but I had no idea so many former employees, business associates, bankers, police, and politicians would attend. Even a few of his enemies showed up to pay their respects. I suspected they were curious to find out who was stepping up to take over the reins of his bootlegging organization. If they expected it to be me, they were sadly mistaken. Or perhaps they were scouting enemy territory and making plans to grab a slice of bootlegger pie for themselves. Either way, I didn't care. I'd long ago made my decision about that way of life.

The Katzenbaum brothers stood with me, one on each side, holding me up both physically and emotionally. Harv and Marv had been my greatest source of stability and advice since the night Will brought me to Mamma's house. Harv Katzenbaum, Gus' attorney, had gone in my place to the morgue and claimed Gus' body. He'd had it transported to the funeral home and made all of the arrangements to spare me any more trauma and grief than I was already going through. Neither brother asked me why I left Gus and went into hiding but I sensed they knew anyway.

In any case, I was grateful for their assistance.

After the funeral ended, Harv and Marv dutifully stood with me, patiently waiting for me to take my leave, but I lingered at the grave for a while. I was reluctant to withdraw from Gus' casket, knowing that once I did, the cemetery staff would cover it with dirt and only his memory would remain. Admittedly, in the last few months, our marriage had fallen apart, but for the last nine years he'd been the center of my world and I found it difficult adjusting to the fact that he was gone *forever*.

Plaguing me the most was that our unborn child would grow up without knowing his father. Someday he would inevitably ask about how Gus had lived and how he had died. How could I tell the truth without spoiling Gus' memory?

"Have you listed the house yet for sale?" I asked Harv, desperate to think about something else. I was content to stay with Mamma for now and had no plans to keep my Summit Avenue residence.

"No," Harv replied quietly. "You'll be moving back there—soon."

Perplexed, I stared at the balding, gray-haired man. "Why in the world would I want to do that?" I whispered. "The place is like a fortress. Too big for one person."

"We need to reinforce your position to equal your husband's status as a successful business owner. You have a lot of responsibility resting on your shoulders now," he whispered back. "You can't run an empire from your mother's place, *Mrs. LeDoux*."

Harv's sharp reply pulled me up short, especially the way he'd formally addressed me. "I helped Gus manage La Coquette. How does that qualify me to take on his entire portfolio?"

"It doesn't. You put your shoulder to the wheel and learn, just like he did. A lot of people are depending upon you for their livelihood."

Gus had a variety of legitimate businesses, such as his car dealership and real estate in addition to his bootlegging activities.

Bootlegging made more money, but he'd used the businesses to launder his illegal gains.

"I can learn to do whatever I put my mind to," I murmured to Harv, "but I want nothing to do with the illegal manufacture, sale, or transportation of liquor."

"As you wish." He glanced around to make sure no one overheard. "Marv and I will take that business over for now."

"We must go over the accounts with you as soon as possible so you're aware of all your enterprises and the schedule of properties you own," Marv whispered, joining in the conversation. His voice sounded a bit rough from chain-smoking Camel cigarettes. "We'll still be making the final decisions for now, but you need to become involved in the day-to-day aspects of management as soon as possible."

I glanced at Marv, wondering why he couldn't wait at least until I'd had the baby. "Is that really necessary?"

"Look around," Marv whispered. "Why do you think so many people have come to Gus' funeral? They're here to find out who has taken the reins of Gus' financial holdings." He gestured toward Leon Goldman, another bootlegger and one of Gus' fiercest enemies. "When they see it's his young wife, they'll say Gus' fortune is doomed. What they don't know is, my brother and I loved Gus like a son and we're not about to let his accomplishments die with him. That's why, *Mrs. LeDoux*, the bootlegger's wife is going to succeed and prove his enemies wrong."

I am? I had no idea why the brothers had so much faith in me.

I sighed and looked down at the grave. "I don't know if I can follow in Gus' footsteps. They're impossibly big."

"Follow our advice," Harv whispered, "and I guarantee you will."

I fell silent, absorbing the enormity of my new role. Could I really do this? As I pondered the idea, I realized I'd already accomplished more in twenty-five years than most people did in a lifetime. Besides, Gus' wealth was our child's inheritance. The money would provide many more opportunities for him than I had growing up in Swede Hollow, but it was up to me now to make sure it was preserved for him.

I looked across the cemetery and saw dozens of men clustered in small groups, talking among themselves. Half of them were probably packing heat underneath their fancy suits.

Leon Goldman caught my eye. The "wheeler-dealer" gangster wore a brown pinstriped suit and a fancy fedora. He looked me over with a patronizing smile and spoke something to his low-life cohorts. The men around him began to look away and conceal their smiles behind their hands. I suspected they were laughing at me, but as far as I was concerned, they were laughing at Gus, too. Not because he'd gotten himself killed, but because he'd left everything in the hands of a *woman*.

Their condescension infuriated me. I stared boldly at the men who had made a joke of me and something inside me irrevocably changed. These people would be watching me, waiting for me to fail and if I did, they'd swoop in to acquire Gus' entities for pennies on the dollar. That was *not* going to happen. I returned Leon's greeting with an innocent smile.

You think I'm ripe for the picking, don't you? A sassy little tart with nothing for brains. I may have grown up poor in Swede Hollow, but I'm not stupid and I know how to fight for what I believe in.

I glanced from my attorney to my accountant. "When do you want me to start?"

If my announcement surprised Harv, he didn't show it. He gave me a stern look. "Tomorrow morning at the office, eight o'clock sharp, and be prepared to *work*."

"I'll be there." I squared my shoulders. "I'm going to give it everything I've got."

"Good," they chanted in unison.

Marv leaned past me and gave his brother a sideways glance. "Hmph. Look who's here."

Harv glanced around surreptitiously, as though trying to figure out which one of St. Paul's notorious criminal figures Marv had spotted. "Who?"

Marv angled his head toward an area on the edge of the crowd. "*Her...*"

I scanned the crowd, curious as to whom they were referring to when I saw her standing alone. Dressed in solid black, the tall, slender woman wore a brimmed hat with a thin veil covering her face, but there was no mistaking my late husband's lover, Adrienne Devereaux.

At first, I stiffened, wondering how she could show her face at this funeral, but the more I studied her, the more I realized her grief was just as real as mine. Besides, at this point, what did it matter that my husband had slept with her? Knowing Gus, she probably wasn't the first, just the first one I'd caught him with. My issues with Gus' infidelity had nothing to do with her and never did.

I touched the edge of Harv's sleeve. "Excuse me for a minute. I need to talk to her."

His eyes widened with alarm. "Don't go over there and make a scene. Just ignore her. I'll have someone remove her."

"Don't do that," I argued. "Adrienne's presence here isn't offensive to me at all. I just want to thank her for coming." I left the brothers mumbling in protest and headed toward her. Harv's cadre of bodyguards followed me like a pack of guard dogs, but I ignored them.

The moment Adrienne realized I was walking toward her she visibly shrank back. I could tell she planned to leave before I reached her to avoid a nasty confrontation. To assure her that I meant no harm, I extended both arms outward, palms up, to project a gesture of acceptance and goodwill. I could tell my actions confused her, and rightly so, but she stayed put until I reached her and took her hands in mine. "Hello, Adrienne. How are you feeling?"

She stared at me through her veil, as though gauging my sincerity. "I'm in shock," she said quietly. "I always knew this day would come. I just never expected it to be so soon. Or so sudden."

The downcast look on her face caused me to wonder if she had any family or friends to provide comfort in her time of need. If so, why hadn't they accompanied her here today?

"I agree," I said somberly. "Life with Gus was difficult at best, but with him gone, it will never be the same."

Trembling, she crushed her handkerchief over her mouth. A tear slid down her cheek. My heart went out to her. Not caring what anyone thought, I put my arms around Adrienne and tried my darnedest to keep from crying myself. "If you ever need anything," I said with a sniffle, "please, just ask me and I'll try to help. If you decide to perform again and need a good reference, I'll provide one for you."

She pulled back, her eyes narrowing with doubt. "After what I did to you, how can you be so forgiving? I don't deserve your kindness."

"You didn't do anything to me," I replied with a stitch in my voice. "It was Gus who betrayed me, not you. I've made my peace with him, so why not you, too?"

"Thank you." She looked relieved as she took my hand and squeezed it. "I was afraid to come today, but now I'm so grateful I did."

"What will you do now?"

She dabbed her nose with the handkerchief. "My future is uncertain. I stopped performing and depended upon Gus for everything because he wanted it that way. Now I have nothing."

It bothered me that Gus had demanded she give up her career for him. A thought came to my mind. "I have a house on Summit Avenue.

There is a guest cottage on the property. If you need a place to stay until you get your life in order, you're welcome to use it."

She blinked with astonishment. "I've seen that house. Gus took me past it once to show me what he'd built. *For you.* It's like a palace. Why aren't you living there?"

"My mamma is not well. For now, I'm staying in her home to take care of her."

"That's very generous of you. I'll give it some thought. Thank you." She smiled and glanced past my shoulder. "I see that handsome detective is here. The one that Gus hired to investigate your disappearance."

"Will? Is here?" I scanned the crowd. "Where?" I hadn't seen or heard from him since the night he brought me to Mamma's house.

Adrienne discretely pointed toward a group of men on the edge of the crowd. I turned my head and saw Will standing near a tree, watching me. As our gazes met, he tipped the brim of his hat, reminding me of how he used to say goodbye when I was his housekeeper.

"I must go," Adrienne whispered in my ear. "Goodbye, dear."

"Goodbye, Adrienne. Take care of yourself."

I turned around and started walking toward Will, hoping to catch him before he left. I wanted to tell him about my interview with Federal agents. They had appeared at Mamma's house the day after Gus' death and asked me pointed questions. I wanted to let Will know it turned out like he'd predicted it would. The agents took my statement, said that was all they needed and never came back.

"Hey, there, Charlie. What's your hurry?"

The voice stopped me dead in my tracks. Only one person called me "Charlie." I slowly turned around and stood face to face with my father, Floyd Johnson. I hadn't seen him since last Christmas. His boozy breath, rumpled suit, and unkempt mop of white hair gave me the impression he hadn't been sober in a long time.

"Hello, Papa. I'm sorry, but I have some pressing business to attend to right now. Why don't we sit down together and talk at the reception?"

"Where's Francie?" he asked, ignoring my answer.

"She's home. Someone has to take care of Mamma." *Remember her? The woman you vowed you'd stick with through sickness and health?* "Excuse me—"

"Before you go," he said hastily and caught me by the arm, "spare your old man a twenty on this fine day. You're holding the purse strings now. Lend your papa a hand."

I should have guessed that was his chief reason for showing up. If Gus were alive, he would have had one of his men—it used to be Albert—put a little bug in Papa's ear. *"Either behave yourself or be gone."*

Disappointed, I gestured toward Marv on the other side of the grave, talking to someone. "I don't have any money on me. Go ask Marv, my accountant, for it. Tell him I said it was okay."

With that, I turned back, intending to sprint straight over to Will. I didn't get far.

He was gone.

* * *

As the months went by, I had my hands full caring for Mamma, dealing with Francie's rebellious growing pains, working with the Katzenbaum brothers, and scheduling doctor appointments while counting down the weeks until my baby was due. Summer turned to fall and my tummy grew until it was a large round ball. I stopped going to Harv's office once my condition became noticeable.

A week before Thanksgiving, I went into labor and gave birth to an eight-pound baby boy, Julien René LeDoux. As I held him in my arms and gazed at his sweet little face, I loved him with every fiber of my being. I'd waited so long for him. It was a dream come true.

Mamma's house was small, so we made the living room into a makeshift nursery. I'd already decided that once I had the baby and got back on my feet, I'd take Harv's advice and move back into the house on Summit Avenue. Until then, I would simply make do where I was. Besides, I wanted Mamma to spend as much time with the baby as she could. Her condition was worsening and I didn't know how much longer she would be with us.

Almost immediately, cards and gifts for my little boy began arriving at the house. Many people came in person to see Gus' son and check on my progress. To my utter delight, one such person was Sally Wentworth. Another was Madeline Van Elsberg.

Madeline arrived on a cold, snowy day in mid-January. She brought a cute little snowsuit for Julien and a bottle of fine wine for me.

"How are you getting along?" Madeline said as she held the sleeping baby in her arms.

"I'm a little cramped here, but this spring I plan to move into a bigger place," I said as I poured coffee for us.

"Little Julien looks just like you. He has your eyes. And he is so long." Madeline peeled back the blanket to reveal the baby's feet protruding from his layette. "He'll probably grow up to be a big man."

I laughed. "I'm only five feet and two inches myself but I'll still be tough enough to handle him even if he grows to be six feet tall."

"Speaking of big guys, have you heard from my brother lately?"

My heart skipped a beat at the reference to Will. "I saw him briefly last summer at the funeral, but we didn't get the chance to talk. Other than that, no. I haven't spoken to him since the day Gus died."

She gave me a sly smile. "He misses you terribly, you know. Oh, he doesn't talk about it, but most men need a little help when it comes to admitting their feelings."

"How do you know that?" I laughed nervously. "...he misses me?"

Madeline handed me the baby and hiked her skirt a couple of inches to retrieve her flask. "Ever since the day you left the house, he's had difficulty concentrating. Peter says that when he's in the office, he spends a lot of time at his desk, staring at the wall."

"That doesn't prove anything."

Madeline unscrewed her flask and poured a shot of whiskey into her coffee. "Their secretary's name is Astrid. Will has slipped up several times and called her *Esther*. The first time, Peter didn't think anything of it because it's an honest mistake, but it happened three times in one month."

"He misses my cooking!" I laughed again, but only to mask my insecurity. I didn't want to hear this. It made me uncomfortable. My husband had only been gone for five months and I'd recently given birth to his child. Besides, as my employer, Will had never been anything but a gentleman around me. The idea of him having *thoughts* about me was absurd.

At least, that's what I told myself.

* * *

In February, I treated Francie to an evening out. We took the streetcar to downtown Minneapolis for dinner and to the theater to see a comedy film called *Girl Shy*, starring Harold Lloyd. Francie had begged me for months to take her to a film and was beside herself with excitement when I agreed to attend this one. I had arranged with Mrs. Olson, our neighbor, to take care of Mamma and Julien for the evening. It was my first time leaving my baby with anyone other than family and though I trusted Mrs. Olson completely, I still couldn't help feeling anxious about being separated from Julien.

Our first stop was at a confectionary to buy a sack of candied walnuts for Mrs. Olson and Demet's Turtles with chocolate, caramel, and pecans for Mamma. Then we went to the Nankin Café for a traditional Chinese dinner. After that, we walked a block and a half to the State Theater on Hennepin Avenue. It was the first time either of us had seen the inside of this theater and as we walked into the wide lobby, I marveled at the sheer beauty of the black and white marble floors, coffered ceilings, and crystal chandeliers.

We went through the open double doors leading to the theater. As I gazed across the huge seating area on the main floor, I'd never seen anything so amazing in my life. The gold proscenium arch curving over the stage was almost as wide as the auditorium itself and stood nearly one hundred feet high. An organist played the Wurlitzer pipe organ, filling the theater with music.

A young usher greeted us wearing a uniform with a short-waisted coat, epaulets, and striped cuffs. He led us down the aisle and showed us to our seats. Much to my embarrassment, Francie openly flirted with him to secure us a pair of seats in the very center of the row. I was only twenty-five, but watching those two made me feel a bit old…

We'd arrived in plenty of time. We took our seats but had to wait a while for the film to begin. I settled in, listening to the music and staring at the hand-painted murals on the walls. I was trying hard to keep myself busy so I would stop obsessing over how much I missed Julien when something caught my eye. I turned my head…

Two rows up, in the seats next to the aisle, Will Van Elsberg relaxed with his arm around a beautiful blonde in a silver fox coat. I knew I shouldn't stare, but I simply couldn't pull my gaze away. I hadn't seen him since that day at the funeral and then only for a brief moment. I must have stared too long because he suddenly turned and glanced my way.

The moment he recognized me his eyes widened. As our gazes

met, something deep and powerful stirred in my heart. The events of our last moments together flashed like a silent film through my mind, pulling me back to that fateful day when Gus' discovery of my whereabouts set off a chain of events no one could stop. I didn't know back then what I'd learned since from Madeline about Will—he'd literally run through a gun battle to find me and save my life. I wondered if my face was as transparent with emotions as his.

Suddenly, the lights went down and the film started. The heavy blanket of darkness disoriented me as I stared in Will's direction, blinking hard, but couldn't see him any longer.

Francie poked me in the ribs, upset that I was leaning across the armrest in my seat and blocking her view. Sitting up straight, I turned toward the screen and stared at the film, but I couldn't concentrate on it. Instead, my mind went back to that day, after Gus' death, vividly remembering the reassuring strength in Will's arms holding me close as we stood in that empty garage and waited out the rain.

It felt as if only a few moments had passed instead of six months.

*   *   *

At the intermission, the lights went up again and everybody began to leave their seats. Francie jumped out of hers and grabbed my hand, anxious to make her way out of the auditorium to avoid standing in a lengthy line in the ladies' room. The crush of people pushing us along made it impossible to stop or even see where we were going, but we eventually made our way out of the auditorium and into the lobby. I maneuvered my way through the throng of people until I found the ladies' room and stood close by, waiting for Francie.

"I like your new hair color," a deep voice murmured in my ear. "It's beautiful."

My heart leaped as I spun around. How he found me in this crowd was a mystery, but I dared to hope he had deliberately looked for me. "Hello, Will. Thank you. I had it dyed back to my natural color. I never really liked it in red."

The first thing I did after the funeral was to have my hair restored to dark brown. I'd gone back to wearing makeup again, as well, although not as much as I used to.

"How have you been?" His warm smile was genuine, but the way he clasped his hands behind his back gave me the sense he was as nervous as I was.

"I'm sick of winter. Other than that, I feel great."

"You look terrific. How's the baby doing? I heard you had a boy."

"Julien is doing well, thank you. He's three months old and growing more every day," I said with a mother's pride. I *loved* talking about my baby. "How about you? Is your new office location working out?"

"Business is good. In fact, I've got more cases than ever. I've promoted Dan to be my assistant." He hesitated. "I understand you're now the big cheese over all of Gus' holdings..."

"Yes. I'm working with the Katzenbaums and I plan to eventually manage everything on my own."

He looked troubled. "There are rumors—that you're—"

"*No*," I emphatically assured him. "Only Gus' legitimate businesses." I shook my head. "I will *never* have anything to do with bootlegging ever again."

He looked relieved. "I'm so glad to hear that, Char. You're a strong woman, but that world is no place for you."

"Sometimes I don't feel very strong, Will. I have dreams about that day. I hear the gunfire and see the shock on Gus' face before he falls—"

"Hey," he said in a low voice and placed his hands on my upper arms, reassuring me with a gentle squeeze. "You were acting in self-defense. Don't blame yourself for Gus' mistakes. Concentrate on raising your little boy instead. Dwell on *his* future, not your past, and the dreams will fade with time." His grip intensified. "Trust me on this."

The clamor of happy theatergoers slowly faded into the background, making it seem as though we were the only people there.

"Words cannot express how grateful I am, Will, for all you did for me that day. You literally saved my life."

"I was desperate to pull you out of harm's way. I couldn't bear to lose you." His eyes searched mine. "I've missed you, Char."

I moved closer, my heart racing. "Then why haven't you called me? You're not the only one with a telephone."

"I wanted to call you," he said tenderly. "You have no idea how badly I've wanted to see you, but I knew you needed time to properly mourn your husband's passing and I didn't want to put any pressure on you. I thought it was best just to stay away."

Will was a man of strong principles, one of the many reasons I admired him, but he wasn't my employer any longer. I was an independent woman who could think for herself. And decide what was best for herself, too.

I lifted my hands to his chest and tugged at the lapels of his jacket. "Did it ever occur to you to *ask me* what I wanted?"

He looked surprised. "I thought I *was* doing what you wanted…" With a slow, gentle motion, he slid his fingers under my chin and lifted it, angling my face closer to his. "So, enlighten me…what *do* you want me to do?"

"I'd love to tell you about it sometime," I replied softly, unable to pull my gaze away from his. "Somewhere more private than this noisy lobby."

The hope in his eyes intensified. "Perhaps over dinner."

"The sooner the better."

"I'm looking forward to it." He flashed a handsome smile. "You decide when. Just say the word—"

I wanted to suggest getting together for dinner tomorrow night, but I didn't get a chance to answer him. The lights began to flicker, announcing the end of the intermission.

"Will!"

From the corner of my eye, I saw his date for the evening emerge from the door of the ladies' room and make a beeline through the crowd toward us. The tall, fur-clad blonde slipped her arm around his, pulling him away from me. Her beautiful, kohl-lined eyes jealously gave me the once-over. "Let's go, darling," she said to Will in a rush. "We need to get back to our seats."

"Goodbye, Will. It was good to see you again," I said as I caught sight of Francie coming out of the ladies' room and started walking toward her.

"The pleasure was all mine." The pointed look in his eyes let me know unequivocally that the conversation was far from over. Bowing his head, he gave me an imaginary tip of his hat. "Give your little boy a hug for me."

A warm glow spread through my body as if I'd been sipping on a premium grade of bootlegged whiskey. He didn't know it yet, but the evening would be spent at his house, just the two of us, with wine, music, dinner and—

I smiled to myself. My mind swirled with plans for our intimate little party, right down to the last detail…

The End (For now…)

The story of Will and Char continues in…

Guarding the Bootlegger's Widow
Book 2 - Moonshine Madness Series

It's 1926 in St. Paul, Minnesota and Prohibition is in full swing. A woman can vote, work full time, show her legs in public and cut her hair but she can't enter a speakeasy without a man by her side…

Charlotte LeDoux is struggling to pick up the pieces of her shattered life. Her late husband, Gus, has left her a lot to deal with—his sprawling business empire, his enemies and an ex-mistress who desperately needs a friend. It's tough for a woman to compete in a man's world and even though it's a never-ending uphill battle, she is determined to succeed.

Char gets a new Model T and is excited when William Van Elsberg offers to give her a driving lesson. She's attracted to the handsome private detective, who, in many ways, is the polar opposite of Gus. Will takes her out for a spin in the car and instructs her how to drive, but at the same time, teaches her how to love again. She's never been so happy!

Meanwhile, Gus' enemies are circling like vultures. An anonymous note threatening Char's life forces Will to become her personal bodyguard. He's highly qualified, but Char's stubborn belief in her own independence makes it the most difficult job he's ever taken. Can he keep her safe or will he lose her in the most dangerous fight of her life?

Also available as an audiobook.

https://www.deniseannettedevine.com

Keep turning the pages for Minnie's Recipes!

Recipes from Minnie's Book

Caramel Pecan Rolls

2 eggs, beaten
1 cup milk, scalded
1 cake yeast
3 1/3 cups flour
¼ cup sugar
1 tsp salt
¼ cup melted shortening/butter mix
Sugar/cinnamon mix

Dissolve yeast, sugar and salt in milk. Add half of the flour, add shortening and remaining flour. Knead. Let rise until doubled. Knead again. Let rise for 10 minutes. Roll flat. Spread with butter. Sprinkle with sugar and cinnamon. Roll and cut.

Caramel Topping

1 cup brown sugar
¼ cup butter
½ cup brown syrup
Pecans

Combine together and melt in a saucepan over low heat. Place in bottom of glass baking pans. Place rolls in pans. Sprinkle with pecans.

Bake 325 – 350 degrees for 20-25 minutes.

Deviled Eggs

8 hard-boiled eggs

¼ to ½ cup mayonnaise (more for creamier version)

1 teaspoon prepared mustard

1 ½ teaspoon sweet or dill relish

salt and pepper (to taste)

paprika or cayenne pepper

Slice eggs in half (lengthwise) and scoop out yolks. Place into a separate bowl. Place whites on a separate plate. Mash yolks. Blend mustard, mayonnaise, and relish into yolks. Fill egg whites with yolk mixture with a spoon. Garnish with a dusting of paprika or cayenne pepper.

Pineapple Skillet Cake

Instead of copying this recipe, I'm posting the link of a site that not only gives you a little history of this wonderful cake, but it also shows you how to make it, step by step with colorful pictures.

https://blog.kingarthurflour.com/2015/03/09/american-baking-decades-1920-1929/

Rhubarb Upside Down Cake

4 tbsp butter

1 ¾ cup sugar

2 cups rhubarb, cut up

2 cups strawberries, sliced

2 eggs

½ cup hot milk

1 tsp baking powder

1 cup flour

¼ tsp salt

½ tsp vanilla

Heat oven to 350 degrees.

Melt 2 tbsp butter and pour into a 9 x 13 baking dish. Add rhubarb and strawberries and ¾ cup sugar. Bake while the batter is being prepared.

Beat eggs 4 minutes at high speed. Add remaining 1 cup sugar, half at a time, and continue beating the batter. Melt remaining butter in milk; sift together (in a separate bowl) flour, salt, and baking powder. Add all gradually to the batter. Pour over hot rhubarb mix and bake for 30 minutes.

Turn over on platter when done.

Sour Cream Cinnamon Coffee Cake

1 stick butter

1 cup sugar

2 eggs

2 cups flour

1 tsp baking powder

1 tsp baking soda

½ pint sour cream

¼ tsp salt

1 tsp vanilla

½ cup finely chopped nuts1/4 cup brown sugar

1 tsp cinnamon

Cream butter and sugar together, beat in eggs. Sift flour, baking powder, baking soda, and salt. Add to butter mixture. Add sour cream and vanilla, mix well. In a separate bowl combine nuts, brown sugar, and cinnamon. Pour a layer of batter into a round, greased tube pan. Spread a layer of the nut mixture and top with a layer of batter.

Bake in a 350-degree oven for 45 minutes.

Sprinkle top with powdered sugar when the cake is cooled.

Underwood Deviled Ham Sandwich Spread
and Chicken Salad

Due to copyright issues, I probably can't include these recipes, so here is the link for you to view them and print them out yourself.

Happy cooking!

https://www.underwoodspreads.com/recipe/deviled-ham-sandwich

A Note from Denise...

The house in Book One is actually a residence that belongs to someone I know. For years, every time I visited the house, my writer's mind kept thinking about how much I wanted to include it in a book. I'd wander from room to room taking pictures. One day an idea clicked in my head and it wouldn't let go until I'd written up a six-page outline. That story sat for two years while I worked on other things, but it was always in the back of my mind. Then one day I knew I *had* to get this story done. By that time, however, one book had developed into three.

I loved writing this book! The characters were so alive for me. Book two (Guarding the Bootlegger's Widow) is also available. I can't wait to get started on the next one and continue their story.

Thank you so much for reading *The Bootlegger's Wife*. If you enjoyed this story, please post a review. Thank you very much!

If you'd like to know more about me or my other books, you can visit my website at:

https://www.deniseannettedevine.com

Like my Facebook page at:

https://www.facebook.com/deniseannettedevine

About the Author

Denise Devine is a USA Today bestselling author who has had a passion for books since the second grade when she discovered Little House on the Prairie by Laura Ingalls Wilder. She wrote her first book, a mystery, at age thirteen and has been writing ever since. She loves all animals, especially dogs, cats, and horses, and they often find their way into her books.

She has written sixteen books, including books in the Beach Brides Series, The Perfect Match Series, and the Hawaiian Holiday Series. Her books have hit the Top 100 Bestseller list on Amazon and she has been listed on Amazon's Top 100 Authors.

Join my reader group - Happily Ever After Stories. If you like sweet romance and want to be part of a great group that has lots of fun and fantastic parties, visit us at:

https://www.facebook.com/groups/HEAstories/.

Other Books by Denise Devine

Christmas Stories
Merry Christmas, Darling
A Christmas to Remember
A Merry Little Christmas
Once Upon a Christmas
A Very Merry Christmas - Hawaiian Holiday Series
~*~

Bride Books
The Encore Bride
Lisa – Beach Brides Series
Ava – Perfect Match Series
~*~

Moonshine Madness Series – Historical Suspense/Romance
The Bootlegger's Wife – Book 1
Guarding the Bootlegger's Widow – Book 2
The Bootlegger's Legacy – Book 3 - Fall 2022
~*~

West Loon Bay Series – Small Town Romance
Small Town Girl – Book 1
Brown-Eyed Girl – Book 2 (September 2022)
~*~

Cozy Mystery
Unfinished Business
Dark Fortune
Shot in the Dark (September 2022)
~*~

This Time Forever - an inspirational romance
Romance and Mystery Under the Northern Lights – short stories
Northern Intrigue – an anthology of mystery stories
~*~

Want more? Read the first chapter of each of my novels on my blog at: https://deniseannette.blogspot.com